Slade's pulse raced. It had been too damn long since he'd held a woman. Since he'd even wanted to...

But Nina had been trembling and afraid. He'd seen the relief in her eyes that finally someone believed her story, and he hadn't been able to resist.

Oh, hell...it was more than that.

She'd fought against all odds to find out what had happened to her baby girl. How could he not admire her dedication and determination?

And now...one touch wasn't enough.

He traced his hand down her hair, then along her cheek.

She tensed slightly as if to pull away, and he tilted her chin up with his thumb.

"I promise you I'll find out what's going on," he said in a deep voice.

She nodded. He traced his finger over her mouth, and her breath hitched, desire flaring in her eyes. "Slade..."

Her raspy sigh was his undoing.

He groaned, then lowered his head, angled his mouth and closed his lips over hers.

Dear Reader,

Twenty-four years ago I gave birth to my third child, a beautiful little girl I named Emily. As I wrote *Unbreakable Bond* she was pregnant with her first baby. Watching the excitement and anticipation as she carried her son brought back precious memories of having my own children and the unbreakable bond between mother and child.

It also reminded me of another special little girl, the *real* Rebecca, the daughter of a very close friend of mine. She was due to be born around the same time as my daughter, but was one of triplets who came prematurely. Sadly, the other two babies didn't make it, but although Rebecca weighed less than a pound and had several health issues, she not only survived, but went on to touch and inspire the lives of everyone around her.

While one would think she might have complained or been a sad child, Rebecca had (and still has) a glow about her.

Unlike the little girl in my story, Rebecca was blessed with two wonderful parents who loved her unconditionally and gave her every opportunity available.

When I see or hear about other challenged children, I often wonder how different it would have been if she hadn't had those parents. And as most mothers, I've thought about how awful it would be for any mother to be separated from her child.

All those elements came together to inspire me to write this story, one I hope will touch you, as well.

So hug your children, love them unconditionally and cherish every precious memory you make together. Children are godsends to us all.

Sincerely,

Rita Herron

RITA HERRON

UNBREAKABLE BOND

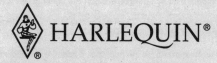

HARLEQUIN®

TORONTO • NEW YORK • LONDON
AMSTERDAM • PARIS • SYDNEY • HAMBURG
STOCKHOLM • ATHENS • TOKYO • MILAN • MADRID
PRAGUE • WARSAW • BUDAPEST • AUCKLAND

To my beautiful daughter Emily
and her new son, Bradford

And to the real Rebecca.
Thanks for inspiring us all!

Recycling programs
for this product may
not exist in your area.

ISBN-13: 978-0-373-74539-5

UNBREAKABLE BOND

ABOUT THE AUTHOR

Award-winning author Rita Herron wrote her first book when she was twelve, but didn't think real people grew up to be writers. Now she writes so she doesn't have to get a *real* job. A former kindergarten teacher and workshop leader, she traded her storytelling to kids for romance, and now she writes romantic comedies and romantic suspense. She lives in Georgia with her own romance hero and three kids. She loves to hear from readers, so please write her at P.O. Box 921225, Norcross, GA 30092-1225, or visit her Web site at www.ritaherron.com.

Books by Rita Herron

*Nighthawk Island
**Guardian Angel Investigations

CAST OF CHARACTERS

Slade Blackburn—Finding missing children is his job—but he can't let his heart get involved.

Nina Nash—Everyone thinks she's crazy, but she believes her daughter Peyton, who police ruled dead, is still alive.

Brooks Nash—Nina's father was upset with her for keeping the baby; does he know more about Peyton's disappearance/death than he's telling?

William Hood—The father of Nina's baby never wanted the child—could he have had the baby kidnapped?

Mitzi Hood—William's wife hated Nina for getting pregnant with his child—would she steal the baby to keep William to herself?

Eileen Hood—William's mother was furious about the child. How far would she go to protect her son's future?

Diane and Dennis Lucas—William's sister and brother-in-law have an eight-year-old daughter who was born around the same time as Peyton. Could the child possibly be Nina's?

Dr. Don Emery—The ob-gyn who delivered Peyton claims there was no way the child survived or was kidnapped. Is he lying?

Paula Emery—Dr. Emery's wife. How far would she go to protect her marriage and money?

Carrie Poole—A nurse on the neonatal unit. Does she know what happened to Peyton?

Stanford Mansfield—Does he arrange illegal adoptions?

Gwen and Roan Waldorp—Gwen gave birth to a stillborn child the night of the fire. Could she have stolen Peyton to replace her own baby?

Prologue

A thunderous boom rocked the hospital walls and floor, jarring Nina Nash awake. What had happened? Had she been dreaming, or had there been an explosion?

Screams and shouts suddenly echoed in the halls, and footsteps of people rushing around outside her room pounded. Somewhere a food cart crashed and glass shattered.

Then the smell of smoke wafted to her.

Panic seized her. Dear God, there *had* been an explosion. The hospital was on fire.

She threw off the covers, not bothering to grab her robe or slip on her bedroom shoes, but the stitches from her C-section pulled as she shuffled to the door and shoved it open. Smoke flooded the hallway in a cloud so thick that she immediately coughed, her eyes watering.

She had to get to her baby. Little Peyton

had been a preemie, less than five pounds, and was in the neonatal intensive care unit.

What if the fire was near the babies?

God, no...

Stumbling forward as fast as she could with her sore abdomen, she heard the sound of voices shouting again, another person crying. The fire alarm trilled, adding to the chaos. Through the gray fog, she spotted patients stumbling outside their rooms, everyone searching for an escape, confused and frightened.

"The east wing is on fire," someone yelled.

"Find the stairwell and get out!" someone else shouted.

"Help me!" a woman screamed.

Someone bumped Nina as they raced down the hall toward the stairwell.

Heat flooded the hall and an orderly grabbed her arm to push her toward the staircase. "This way, miss."

"No, I have to get to my baby," Nina cried.

"No time, the nurses and firefighters are getting the infants out! And that corridor is engulfed in flames."

"Then I'll find another way," she said and tore away from him.

Another woman darted into the fog of smoke, coughing as she collapsed onto the floor, and the rescue worker rushed to help her.

Determined to save Peyton, Nina hurried down the hall. But just as she reached the end, the ceiling crashed down, and flames shot all along the wall and floor, blocking the turn into the corridor.

She pivoted and headed in the opposite direction, feeling along the wall until she reached the next corner, but the smoke was so thick she could barely see, and flames rushed toward her. No… There was no way to get through….

Tears mingled with the sweat on her face as the heat scalded her. She had to try another direction.

Coughing, she dashed back the way she'd come, but suddenly another explosion rocked the building, the floor shook, and the ceiling crashed down.

Nina covered her head to dodge the debris, but plaster rained down on her, and a piece of metal slammed into her head. Another pummeled her leg and foot, and ceiling tiles smashed into her stomach, ripping open stitches. Pain rocked through her, and she screamed as she collapsed onto the floor. The scalding flames crawled toward her.

Through the haze, more footsteps rumbled, then a firefighter appeared and scooped her up. "My baby," she cried. "I have to get her."

"We'll find her," he said. "Just let me take you outside before the whole wing is engulfed in flames."

Tears trickled down her cheeks as he carried her through the blazing hallway, dodging flames and more falling debris. She gulped in the fresh air as he burst out the front door and raced down the steps to the lawn. Blinking her stinging eyes to clear her vision, she searched the haze and chaos.

Firefighters were scrambling to help victims and extinguish the flames, but at least half the hospital was ablaze. Patients, hospital employees, doctors, nurses and visitors ran, crawled and helped each other from the burning building.

She spotted one of the neonatal nurses unconscious on a gurney, and two nurses holding infants, and hope shot through her. The firefighter carried her toward an ambulance, but she pushed against his chest. "Let me down."

"Ma'am, you need to see a medic. You've been injured."

She didn't care if her head was bleeding, that her stitches had popped or her leg was throbbing. She had to make sure her daughter was safe. "No, not until I find my baby."

She managed to get on her feet, then stumbled toward the nurses. But her heart sank when she realized neither of the babies was Peyton.

"Where's my little girl?" she cried. "She was in the neonatal unit."

One of the nurses frowned, and the other one shook her head with worry. "I'm not sure. Maybe one of the other nurses got her."

Another baby's cry rent the air, and she turned and raced toward the sound. A medic was holding the infant, but when she neared him, she realized the baby was a boy.

Panic clawed at her, and she ran from medic to medic, from nurse to doctor to orderly. Screams and cries flowed freely as people were carried from the hospital and the body count began to rise. More sirens and cries reverberated as police, friends and relatives of the hospital employees and patients arrived, each searching for loved ones.

Finally she found one of the nurses who'd cared for Peyton lying on another stretcher, and she hobbled toward her. "Where's my baby?"

Sorrow filled the nurse's eyes as she looked at Nina. "I don't know. I thought someone else rescued her."

The sound of the NICU exploding rent the air, and Nina's legs gave way, a sob of terror ripping from her.

Dear God…

Where was her baby?

Chapter One

Eight years later

Finding missing children was the only thing that kept Slade Blackburn going. The only thing that kept him from giving into the booze that promised sweet relief and numbness from the pain of his failures.

That was, when he found the children alive.

The other times…well, he locked those away in some distant part of his mind to deal with later. *Much,* much later when he was alone at night, and the loneliness consumed him and reminded him that he didn't have a soul in the world who gave a damn if he lived or died.

Voices echoed through the downstairs as the agents at Guardian Angel Investigations entered the old house Gage McDermont had converted into a business and began to climb the stairs.

Slade's instincts kicked in. He'd arrived early, situated himself to face the doorway in the conference room so he could study each man as he entered.

Not that he hadn't done his research.

Gage had started the agency in Sanctuary and recruited an impressive team of agents.

The moment Slade had read about GAI in the paper, he'd phoned Gage and asked to sign on. Leaving his stint in the military had left him wired and honed for action, yet the confines of the FBI or a police department had grated on his newfound freedom.

Too long he'd taken orders, followed commands. Now he was his own man and wanted no one to watch over, not as he'd had to do with his combat unit.

But he needed a case.

Bad.

Being alone, listening to the deafening quiet of the mountains, remembering the horrific events he'd seen, was wreaking havoc on his sanity.

He refused to be one of those soldiers who returned from war damaged and suffering from post-traumatic stress syndrome.

He would not fall apart and become needy, dammit.

And he *would* keep the nightmares at bay.

By God, he'd survived his childhood and Iraq, and he wouldn't go down now.

Still, returning to the small town of Sanctuary, North Carolina, held its own kind of haunts, and when he'd passed by Magnolia Manor, the orphanage where his mother had dropped him off without looking back, he'd questioned his decision to settle in the town.

Gage McDermont strode in and took the head seat behind the long conference table while the others filed in. Slade maintained his stoic expression, honing his self-control.

Gage gestured toward Slade. "This is Slade Blackburn," he said. "He just finished his first case and returned Carmel Foster's runaway daughter to her."

The men surrounding the table nodded, then Gage gestured to each of them as he made the introductions. Slade analyzed each one in turn.

Benjamin Camp, a dirty-blond-haired computer expert with green eyes. Brilliant techy, he'd heard. Slade would bet he had a shady past. Maybe a former criminal with skills that could come in handy in a pinch.

Levi Stallings, former FBI profiler, black hair, military-style haircut, dark brown eyes. Intense, a man who studied behaviors and got into a killer's mind. He cut his gaze toward Slade as if dissecting him under his microscope, and Slade forced himself not to react, to meet him with an equally hard stare.

First rule of engaging with the enemy: *Never let on that you're afraid or intimidated.*

Not that he was, but he didn't like *anyone* messing with his mind or getting too close.

Adopting his poker face, he angled his head to study the man, seated next to him, whom Gage introduced as Brock Running Deer.

"Running Deer is an expert tracker," Gage said in acknowledgment.

A skill that would be needed in the dense mountains. He was also big, slightly taller than Slade's own six feet, had shoulder-length brown hair, auburn eyes and was part Cherokee. He scowled at Slade as if he were permanently angry, but Slade shrugged it off. He hadn't come here to make friends.

"And this is Derrick McKinney."

Slade nodded toward him.

Next Gage introduced Caleb Walker, who also looked mixed heritage. He had thick black hair, black eyes, and wore a guarded expression. Gage didn't elaborate on his particular skill, which made Slade even more curious about the man.

Gage gestured to the last man seated around the table. "This is Colt Mason, a guns and weapon expert." Slade sized him up. Short, spiked black hair, crystal-blue eyes, sullen and quiet. He had that military look about him, as well, as if he'd stared down death and it hadn't fazed him. Probably former Special Ops.

The door squeaked open and a petite brunette with hair dangling to her waist and large brown eyes slipped in.

Gage's face broke into a smile. "This is Amanda Peterson, our newest recruit. Amanda is a forensics specialist, and we're glad to have her on board.

"Now that we've all been introduced, I want to get you up to speed on the latest case and the arrests made in Sanctuary. Brianna Honeycutt, now the wife of Derrick, adopted an infant son when the baby's mother, Natalie Cummings, was murdered. Our investigation revealed that Natalie learned about a meth lab in town that was connected to the creators of a lab eight years ago, the one that caused the hospital fire and explosion that took dozens and dozens of lives."

Gage paused and twisted his mouth into a frown. "The police have made several arrests, but locals are up in arms now that they know who was responsible. There's also been speculation that there might have been more locals involved in the lab. Lawsuits are cropping up each day, and people who lost loved ones are asking questions. Due to the fire and contamination of evidence, there are questions regarding some of those who were presumed dead."

Slade frowned. "Presumed?"

"Ones whose bodies were never found or identified," Gage clarified. "Among those were women and children. I expect that we might have some work ahead of us."

Slade's blood began to boil. Women and children…who'd died because of some stupid drug lab. Women and children whose bodies had never been identified.

Families with no answers just as his own hadn't had answers when his older sister had disappeared. Not until Slade had found her in the morgue.

Maybe it was right that he'd come back to Sanctuary. If he had the opportunity to find closure for even one of the families involved, it was worth it.

Then maybe he could finally find peace and forgive himself for his sister's death.

NINA'S BABY'S CRY HAUNTED her every day.

Peyton would have been eight years old had she survived, the same age as the children Nina taught at Sanctuary Elementary.

She tried to envision what her daughter would look like now as she watched her students rush to the school bus, squealing and laughing, excited to be out for summer break. Most of the teachers were jumping for joy, as well.

"Freedom at last," one third-grade teacher said with a laugh.

"Vacation," another one boasted.

But instead of dreaming about long, lazy days at home or a vacation road trip, tears filled Nina's eyes.

To her, summer break meant weeks of being without the kids. Long, lonely days and nights of silence. Of no tiny hands reaching out for help, no sweet voices calling her name, no little patter of feet or giggles, no little arms wrapping around her for a big bear hug.

Tortured nights of an empty house and more nightmares of what her life would have been like if her little girl were alive.

For a moment, she allowed herself to dream of taking her daughter to the beach. They'd build sand castles, collect shells, ride bikes.

She could almost hear her daughter's laughter in the wind roaring off the ocean….

The bus driver gave a big honk of its horn, jerking her back to reality. Kids waved and screamed out the window, and the bus roared away. Teachers cheered and waved, laughing and talking about their plans as they dispersed back to their rooms to tidy up for the day.

Nina wrapped her arms around her waist and watched until the last bus disappeared from the school drive, then turned and walked back inside, her chest tight.

She should be over the loss of her daughter, people had told her. "Move on with your life," her father had insisted. "Let it go," the ob-gyn had said.

But sometimes at night, she heard her baby's cries, and she sensed that Peyton was still alive. That she hadn't died in that fire. That she was out there somewhere, and that she needed her.

Moving on autopilot, she went to her classroom, packed up boxes, wiped down the chalkboard, stripped the bulletin boards and cleaned out her desk.

Finally she couldn't procrastinate any longer. The empty room was almost as sad and overwhelming as her house. Here she could still see the kids' cherub faces, hear their chatter and smell their sweet, little bodies.

She stuffed her worn plan book in her favorite tote, one emblazoned with a strawberry on the front and sporting the logo Teachers Are Berry Special, then added a copy of the language arts guide for the new language arts program the county had adopted, threw the tote over her shoulder, flipped off the lights and headed outside.

The late-afternoon sunshine beat down on her as she walked to the parking lot. The sound of engines starting up filled the air, and she noticed a group of teachers gathering for an end-of-the-year celebration.

Celia, her friend from the classroom across the hall from her, looked up and waved as she climbed in her minivan. Celia had invited her to join them, but she'd declined. Celebrating was the last thing on her mind.

Instead she drove to the little bungalow she'd bought in town, picked up the newspaper on the front stoop, then dragged herself inside and poured a glass of sweet iced tea. Hating the silence that engulfed her, she flipped on the television, then glanced at the front page of the paper.

The headlines immediately caught her eye. *Murder of Natalie Cummings and Kid-*

napping of Her Son Ryan Leads to Answers about the Hospital Explosion and Fire Eight Years Ago.

Nina skimmed the article, her own memories of the explosion taunting her. For years now the town had mourned the lives lost back then. Now they finally had answers.

Police have learned that a meth lab built by local teenagers at the time was the cause of the explosion that killed dozens. Recently Natalie Cummings had overheard students at Sanctuary High discussing a new meth lab nearby, and she was apparently murdered when she connected the current lab to the one eight years ago.

Derrick McKinney, an agent from Guardian Angel Investigations, was instrumental in uncovering the truth about the explosion, the kidnapping and murder connection.

Nina frowned, her heart racing. That night had been horrible. The explosion, the fire, the terrible confusion. The burning bodies.

Her frantic rush to find Peyton…

Her stomach knotted. She'd wondered if her baby might have been confused with another that night, or if she could have been kidnapped in the chaos.

But the investigation had been a mess, and the sheriff had assured her her fears had been unfounded. Even worse, the P.I. she'd hired had been convinced she was just a hysterical mother and had done nothing but take her money.

Still, one question nagged at her. They had never found Peyton's body.

She glanced at the article again. *Guardian Angel Investigations.* They specialized in finding missing children.

Her hand shook as she went to the mantel and picked up the photo of her newborn. Peyton had been so tiny Nina had been able to hold her in one hand.

If someone had kidnapped her, how would she have survived?

Still, every night when she crawled into bed, she heard her cries. And every time she closed her eyes, a little angel's voice sang to her in the night.

Determination and a new wave of hope washed over her as she grabbed her purse. "I'm going to find you, baby."

If GAI had dug deeply enough to find out who'd caused that fire, maybe they could dig even deeper and find out what had happened to her daughter.

JUST AS THE MEETING was about to disperse, the bell on the downstairs door jangled. Gage gestured for the group to wait while he descended the stairs. A minute later, he returned, escorting a young woman with him.

A beautiful blonde with long wavy hair, enormous blue eyes the color of the sky on a clear North Carolina day, and a slim body with plump breasts that strained against her soft, white blouse.

But nothing about the woman indicated she was aware of her beauty.

Instead, those blue eyes looked wary and were filled with the kind of grief and sadness that indicated she'd lived through a hell of her own.

"This is Nina Nash," Gage said. "She's interested in our services."

Gage gestured for her to sit down, and Slade noticed her body trembling slightly as she slid into a leather chair. Why was she on edge?

Was she intimidated by the agents, or in some kind of trouble?

"How can we help you, Miss Nash?" Gage asked.

She bit down on her lower lip and twisted her hands together, glancing at each of them as if to decide whether to continue.

"Just relax and tell us your story," Gage said in a soothing tone.

She nodded, then jutted up her little chin, took a deep breath and spoke. "I read about your agency in the paper and saw that you found the people responsible for the hospital fire and explosion eight years ago."

"Yes," Gage said. "The police made some arrests."

"I…lost my baby that night," Nina said in a pained tone. "At least she went missing."

A hushed silence fell across the room as everyone contemplated her statement. Finally Gage assumed the lead and spoke. "Why don't you start from the beginning and tell us what happened."

She rolled her tiny hands into fists as if to hold herself together. "My baby girl was early, a preemie, and I had to have a C-section," she said as if she'd repeated this story a thousand times already. Then she rushed on as if she had to spit it out or she'd completely crumble. "I was asleep when the sound of the explosion woke me. Everyone started shouting and screaming, and I smelled smoke so I got out of bed and tried to get to the nursery, to Peyton…" Her voice cracked in the deafening silence stretching across the room.

But no one spoke. Her anguish was like a palpable force in the room.

"It was chaos," she said on a choked breath. "Everyone was screaming, desperate to escape. Patients were struggling and needing help, and an orderly told me to go to the stairwell, but I couldn't leave my baby so I pushed him away."

She hesitated and drew a shaky breath. "Smoke filled the halls, but I ran toward the corridor leading to the neonatal intensive care unit, but it was on fire, and I couldn't get past, so I tried the other way, then the ceiling crashed and debris was falling and I was hit…"

She swiped at a tear that trickled down her cheek, and Slade sucked in a sharp breath. Others shifted restlessly.

"I fell and was bleeding and a fireman carried me outside, but I wouldn't let them treat me. I ran through the crowd searching for my baby. I found two nurses holding infants, but none of them was Peyton…" A shudder ripped through her body. "Then the building crashed down in flames."

Slade knew the answer, but he asked the question anyway. "Did they find your baby's body?"

She shook her head no. "The scene was a

mess. It took hours for the firefighters to control the blaze. Later the police said my baby must have died when the building crashed, that it would probably take months for the medical examiner to sort through the bodies." Her mouth tightened, then she looked up with steely determination in her eyes. "They never found her. And I know she didn't die that night." She pressed her hand to her chest. "I know it in my heart, and I want you to look for her."

"Nina," Gage said quietly. "I understand your grief, but if Peyton had lived, don't you think the hospital would have informed you?"

"I don't know," she said in a quivering voice. "It was so chaotic that night, someone could kidnapped her, or she could have gotten switched with another baby."

Caleb Walker cleared his throat. "You had a breakdown afterward, didn't you, Nina?" His tone was low, not accusatory but understanding. "And you saw a woman who claimed to be a medium. You tried to communicate with your little girl, but it didn't work."

She clenched her jaw. "Yes," she admitted. "But I'm *not* crazy. I'm not. I can hear her cries sometimes at night. I'm her mother, I have instincts. We bonded." Another tear escaped but she didn't bother to wipe it away this time.

Slade gripped the arm of the chair to keep himself from going to her and wiping it away.

"Peyton would be eight years old now," she said, her voice growing stronger with conviction. "I know she's out there and she needs me."

Skeptical looks passed quietly around the room. Nina obviously noticed because she stood, anger sizzling in her eyes.

For some reason he didn't understand, Slade couldn't let her leave. Not yet. "You hired a P.I. before?"

She nodded and hissed in frustration—or rage. "But he didn't believe me. He just took my money, then told me I was stupid to keep searching." Her voice rose another decibel. "But how can I not look for my little girl when I think she might be alive? It would be as if I abandoned her."

Slade gritted his teeth. Plenty of mothers did just that.

She jammed her hands on her hips. "Everyone thought that fire was an accident, and GAI proved it wasn't. Why can't you believe that my baby might be alive, that someone might have taken her that night? Why can't you at least just look into it?"

Because they all knew the infant had probably died in the fire, Slade thought. But he refrained from saying it, and so did the others.

"With all the revelations you've uncovered about that fire, about people in the town covering up the reason for the explosion," Nina continued, pressing, "maybe someone knows something about my baby."

Slade considered the possibility. The town had kept its secrets and people had suffered for it.

He'd also seen and heard bizarre stories before, knew that people could be devious. Gage had indicated that there might be more locals who'd known the truth about that night but hadn't come forward. That there might have been more people involved.

Nina's theory that someone could have kidnapped her baby in the chaos actually sounded feasible. If there was a chance that she was right and her child was alive, how could they not investigate?

Chapter Two

Nina recognized the skepticism in the room, and frustration welled inside her. She'd been a fool to come here, to hope that someone would finally listen to her.

That they would open a case that had been closed for nearly a decade—actually a case that had never been opened.

Even her own father thought she'd lost her mind and that she should let it go.

It was the reason she hadn't spoken to him in months.

She glanced at the only female in the room, hoping she'd at least piqued her interest enough to take on the investigation, but pity darkened her eyes and she made no offer.

Irritated at them all, and with herself for thinking she might have found an ally in this group, she gritted her teeth. "Fine, if you won't help me, I'll ask around again myself." Although she knew that would lead her nowhere.

Most of the people she'd talked to knew her story and thought she should get psychological help, not a detective.

She had just reached the doorway when one of the men said, "I'll take the case."

Uncertain that she'd heard him correctly, she froze and slowly turned around. The intense man who'd sat next to Gage McDermont stood. "My name is Slade Blackburn, Miss Nash. I'll look into your child's disappearance."

Nina blinked in stunned shock. Of all the men at the table, he'd acted the coldest, looked the hardest. He was tall and big, his broad shoulders stretching the confines of his black button-up shirt. Jeans hugged his thighs, thighs that looked like tree trunks compared to her own.

Her gaze fell to the scar down the left side of his cheek, a knife wound that had to have been done fairly recently. Tousled brownish-black hair fell across one eye, and he swept it back with his hand. A hand also scarred with a jagged cut.

This man looked intimidating, impressive, like a fighter.

"Slade," Gage began, but the man cut him off with a dismissive gesture that seemed to surprise his boss.

"You don't have another case you need me on right now, do you, boss?"

"No," Gage said. "But you just returned from one. I figured you might want some time off."

"No," Slade said in a deep take-charge tone. "I came here to work. I like to stay busy."

The woman spoke up next. "We'll help any way you need us."

A chorus of agreements and nods followed, and Nina finally released the breath she'd been holding. "Thank you."

Slade didn't acknowledge her thanks. Instead, he gestured toward the door. "I'd like to talk to you in private, ask you some more questions."

Nina's chest tightened. Searching for Peyton would mean opening old wounds, but she had to suck up her pride.

She'd do anything to find her daughter.

SLADE ESCORTED NINA to his office and gestured for her to sit. "Would you like coffee or some water?"

Her delicate body collapsed into the chair as if she were too weary to stand any longer, and the temptation to comfort her hit him.

But that would be a mistake.

"Water, please," she said in a low voice.

He disappeared for a moment, went to the kitchen then returned with coffee for himself and a bottle of water for her. By the time he walked in, she'd straightened her shoulders as if regaining control and bracing for an interrogation.

His suspicions mounted. What was she hiding?

"All right," she said. "What did you want to ask me?"

He offered a small smile as he settled at his desk, hoping to relax her, but she clenched the water bottle in a death grip.

"I need some background information," he said, then reached for a legal pad and pen. "Tell me the date of your daughter's birth. And her name."

"I named her Peyton," she said, then gave him the date and time of her birth. The realization that she'd counted the birthdays since made compassion twitch at his veneer.

"You said she was in the NICU?"

"Yes, she was premature," Nina said. "A seven-month baby. She had trouble breathing at first, and weighed a little over four pounds."

His gaze shot to hers. "Any other problems?"

"She was only a day old. The doctors

planned to run more tests… They thought she might have had vision problems…"

Slade swallowed. If someone had kidnapped this preemie, and she had had health issues, she might not have survived afterward. He needed to check old police reports to see if any premature infants had been abandoned around that time.

Or if any infants' bodies had been found.

Damn. The thought made his own stomach roil. He couldn't imagine the torture this woman had suffered. The fear, the horror stories of other abandoned babies she'd heard about on the news, the not knowing or thinking that each time an infant's body had been discovered that it might be hers…

Forcing his mind back to his job, he glanced at her ring finger, but it was bare. No tan line where a wedding ring might have been either.

"Who was the baby's father, and is he still in the picture?"

She glanced down at her hands. "His name was William Hood. He was nineteen, and I was eighteen at the time. And no, he's not in the picture."

"Tell me what happened between you."

Her gaze flew to his, anxiety lining her

face. "Is it really necessary for me to go into this?"

Slade leaned forward, his arms on the desk, his expression neutral. "I know this is difficult, but you came to me for help, Nina. If you want me to investigate, I need to know everything about that time in your life." He swallowed. "And I mean *everything*. So don't hold back or lie to me or I'm off the case."

Anger glittered in her eyes, but she gave a nod. "All right."

"How did William react to the pregnancy?"

"Not well. He had a scholarship to Duke, and didn't want his life interrupted."

"But your life was," he said calmly.

A tiny smile slowly softened her eyes. "Yes. Even though I was young and the pregnancy was a surprise, I really wanted the baby. I felt connected to her immediately." Her hand automatically went to her stomach, and an image of a young, naive girl flashed in his head.

One who would have made a wonderful mother.

Slade tried to ignore the feelings that realization stirred.

"So, what did William do? Did he refuse to accept responsibility?"

Nina's mouth thinned again. "Pretty much. He and his parents tried to convince me to have an abortion." A shudder rippled through her. "His mother even offered me a bribe to leave town and get rid of the baby."

Slade studied her for a moment. "Did any of them threaten you?"

Nina frowned as if thinking back. "Not in so many words, although Mrs. Hood warned me that I'd be sorry if I ruined her son's life. William's father had died the year before, and she wanted William to follow in his footsteps and become a lawyer."

Slade tamped back his anger. "What did you say to her?"

"I let them all off the hook," Nina said calmly. "I told them I didn't want their money, that I didn't need or want William, and that they could all go to hell."

Admiration stirred in Slade's chest. "Have you heard from him lately?" Slade asked.

"No. I did hear that he got married to a former girlfriend, a debutante named Mitzi. I'm sure his mother was thrilled."

"What about your family?"

Anguish flickered in her eyes momentarily before she blinked away the emotion. "I lost my mother when I was little. My father was upset with me about the pregnancy. He also tried to convince me to abort the baby, then insisted if I kept her, that I should give her up for adoption." She uncapped the water bottle and took a long sip, then set it down and looked at him again. "He thought I was too young and irresponsible to raise a child. And when the doctors declared that Peyton died in that hospital fire, he assured me it was for the best."

Slade gritted his teeth. Was her father simply protective, or a bastard with an insensitive heart?

"He didn't believe that your daughter might still be alive?"

She made a sound of disgust. "No, he actually seemed relieved. He thought I was crazy and insisted I go into therapy."

"Because he loved you," Slade said.

Another sound of disgust. "That's what he said. That I was better off that my little girl died." She turned an anguished look his way. "How could anybody say that? That it was God's way of giving me a second chance at a normal life?" Her voice quivered again. "All I wanted was my baby back."

"Maybe he was trying to help," Slade suggested.

She shook her head. "No, he was embarrassed that I had an illegitimate child, worried about what it would do to his precious reputation." She looked down at her hands where she'd twined them in her lap. "He didn't give a damn about Peyton."

He let her words sink in. So her father was relieved to have the child out of the way. He already disliked the man. "And you did go to college?"

She nodded. "Not at first, but eventually I pulled myself together and earned a teaching degree. Now I teach second grade at Sanctuary Elementary." Her eyes softened again as if being around the children helped alleviate her suffering.

Slade considered her mental condition and hated the doubts assailing him. Needing to know the truth was one thing. Obsession to the point of stalking, another animal instead. "You stayed in Sanctuary because you thought your daughter might be here, didn't you?" Slade asked. "You looked for her in every child in school and in town."

But she didn't hide her motives or defend herself. She nodded instead, tears blurring her eyes. "I know that sounds pathetic, but I just felt close to her here."

Just as his mother had refused to move from their home after his sister had disappeared. She'd claimed that she had to be at the house in case his sister returned. Eventually, though, her obsession had driven her over the edge....

"No," Slade said evenly. "I understand."

Her eyes narrowed, and her voice dropped to a whisper. "You do?"

Unable to resist, he reached out and covered her hands with his own. "My sister disappeared from our house when I was fifteen. For days and months afterward, I looked for her in every teenager I spotted."

"You found her?" Nina asked.

God, he didn't want to answer that. Didn't want to shatter any ounce of hope she had. But the truth could be brutal sometimes.

"Yes," he finally answered. "But we didn't have a happy ending, Nina. She was in the morgue."

Nina inhaled a sharp breath. "I'm sorry," she said, then squeezed his fingers. "What happened?"

Hell, he'd already said too much. And she was looking at him with such compassion that emotions he'd long thought buried pummeled him.

No. He couldn't, *wouldn't* blurt out the rest.

"You don't want to know." He cleared his throat. "But think long and hard about this,

Nina," he said gruffly. "What will you do if we investigate and find out that your baby did die in that fire? Are you prepared for that reality?"

NINA'S CHEST ACHED from trying to maintain control. Slade's question threatened to shatter that control.

Was she prepared? How would she respond if he discovered that Peyton really had died? All these years she'd lived on the belief that her little girl was out there needing and wanting her.

"How can I not find out the truth?" she finally said. "I need closure, Mr. Blackburn."

"Slade," he said automatically. "And are you sure it's closure you want? She might be gone forever."

Pain rocked through her, but she cloaked herself in the coat of armor she'd donned years ago. She would survive no matter what. "I realize that, but not knowing is no way to live."

He studied her with such an intensity that she was tempted to squirm. But she refused to show weakness or he might decide she was the nutcase her father and Dr. Emery thought.

He gave a brisk nod. "All right. But what if someone did kidnap your baby, and she's been adopted and is now happy? What will you do then?"

She had considered that theory, but somehow in her heart she knew that wasn't the case. "She needs me," she said simply. "I'm her mother. I feel it."

A muscle ticked in his jaw. "You have to consider every scenario, Nina. What if she has loving parents and doesn't know anything about you? What if she has a family that she loves?"

"I don't know," she said softly, honestly. "I guess I'll cross that bridge when, or if, we come to it. But I am her mother and I deserve to know where she is."

"Fair enough." Slade nodded, then released her hand.

Odd how she hadn't leaned on anyone in years, but for a moment, she'd felt as if she had someone on her side now.

Someone she trusted. And after her father's and William's betrayals, she'd never trust anyone again.

SLADE HAD HIS WORK cut out for him. Even though Nina insisted she could handle the truth, no matter what he discovered, he understood the emotional roller-coaster ride involved in looking for a missing child. The toll it took could be dangerous.

His mother certainly hadn't survived the ride.

And judging from Nina's fragile looks, she'd been surviving on hope for years. If he stripped that hope, she might crash and burn just as his mother had.

Then again, beneath that tenderness, she was stubborn. Determined. And he also understood the torture not knowing caused.

She licked her lips, drawing his attention to her mouth, and a foreign feeling bled through him, one he didn't want. He itched to draw her tiny hand back into his, kiss it and promise her that he would make things right.

His body reacted, hardened, betraying his better sense and reminding him that his libido wasn't dead after all. Geesh, a fine time for it to burst back to life.

Fortunately she didn't seem to notice.

"Where do we start?" she asked.

Reining in his sudden bout of lust, he forced his mind back to the case. "I'll put out some feelers across the States, search the National Center for Missing and Exploited Children Web site, check into adoptions that occurred around the time of the fire. I'll question nurses, hospital staff and other locals at the scene that night." He hesitated. "I'll also have to question your father, and William Hood and his family."

"They won't be happy that I've opened this up again," Nina said.

Slade shrugged. He already didn't like her father or the Hoods. "I don't give a damn who I piss off, Nina. I'm on the case now, and I will find out exactly what happened to your baby girl."

He just hoped to hell she could handle the truth when he did.

Chapter Three

Fatigue from dredging up the past pulled at Nina, but hope fluttered wildly in her chest. Slade would be opening up old wounds between her and her father, and her and the Hoods, but she'd survived their disdain before and she would again.

At least someone was finally going to ask questions.

"Does your father live in town?" Slade asked.

"No, he's in Raleigh." She gave him her father's contact information, including his work number at the bank. "I'm out of school for the summer and want to accompany you when you talk to him."

He arched a brow. "Are you sure that's a good idea?"

No, but she wanted to see her father's reaction. "I can handle it."

He gave a clipped nod. "What about William and his family?"

"They're in Winston-Salem. William took over his father's law practice there."

Slade jotted down the name of the firm, then ran his hand through his hair. "What was the name of the doctor who delivered your baby?"

Fresh pain burned her stomach at the mere mention of his name. The delivery had been harrowing enough, but he had been a strong proponent of adoption. "Dr. Don Emery."

"Does he still live and practice in Sanctuary?"

"Yes, I think so, although I haven't seen him in months. I tried to talk to him several times, but like everyone else, he encouraged me to move on."

Slade's mouth tightened slightly. "I know this is difficult, but think back to the night of the delivery and the day after. Did you notice anything strange, anyone suspicious at the hospital?"

"God, I was so scared that night and was in such a panic, that I don't remember much. Just that I knew my baby was coming too early, and that I was afraid for her."

"You were in labor?"

She nodded. "I'd developed complications.

They rushed me to the operating room and took her immediately." Her heart quickened at the memory. "She wasn't breathing at first, and they had to give her oxygen. She was so tiny and weak that I didn't know if she'd make it…"

His eyes held compassion as she paused to pull herself together.

"What about the next day? Did you notice someone watching the nursery, looking at the babies?"

Nina massaged her temple as she struggled to force the details of the hospital stay to the surface. "Not that I recall."

"Did anyone make an odd comment to you about keeping the baby?"

Nina grimaced. "Dr. Emery agreed with my father and encouraged me to give Peyton up for adoption. They both thought that she needed two parents. A couple of nurses also mentioned that adoption might be a good idea."

"Do you remember those nurses' names?"

Nina rubbed her temple again. "I don't know last names, but one nurse was Jane and the other Carrie. I saw both of them outside the hospital after the fire, but they claimed they didn't know where Peyton was."

Slade frowned. Was it possible someone had taken the baby from the nursery before it caught on fire?

SLADE BIT BACK HIS thoughts. He hated offering Nina false optimism.

"So where do we start?" she asked.

Slade checked his watch. "It's already getting late. I'll start putting out contacts on the Internet tonight, call a couple of friends who might be able to help look into the adoption angle, and drop by the hospital and see if the administrator and Dr. Emery are there." He paused. "Tomorrow I'd like to talk to your father and meet the Hood family."

Nina gripped the armrest. "Let's get started."

Slade sighed. "Nina, why don't you go home tonight and rest."

"No," she said in a pleading tone. "I know this is difficult for you to understand, but I feel…lost in that house alone right now."

Hell, the trouble was he *did* understand. He knew how the silence could eat at you, how a person's absence could feel like part of you had been ripped out. How the walls could scream at you with recriminations.

"All right," he said gruffly. "But remember, we may not find anything."

She took another sip of water, then wiped her mouth. "Thanks. I appreciate your candor."

"Let me talk to Derrick, then we'll head to the hospital." He stood, then strode down the hall to McKinney's office.

Derrick was on the phone when he knocked, but ended the call and gestured for him to enter.

"I need to ask you a favor," Slade said bluntly.

Derrick pointed to the chair beside his desk. "You're taking on the case for Nina Nash?"

Slade took the chair. "Yes."

Derrick frowned. "You know that baby may not have survived."

Slade's gut knotted. "I know. But after hearing Nina's story, it's possible that someone could have kidnapped the baby in the chaos."

Derrick folded his arms. "What can I do to help?"

"Talk to your wife, Brianna, for me."

Derrick arched a brow. "How do you know Bri?"

"I lived at Magnolia Manor when I was a teenager for a while. We met there. I heard she's a social worker now with an adoption agency."

The realization of where he was headed dawned in Derrick's eyes. "She was," Derrick said. "But she's taken a leave of absence to stay home with the baby."

"But Brianna has contacts, right?" Slade asked.

"Probably." Derrick narrowed his eyes. "You know that adoption records are sealed?"

"Yes, but Brianna must have a friend who can look back through files quietly. Nina's baby was premature, and had trouble breathing. Handling an adoption for a preemie with medical problems would be tricky—and memorable."

"That's true," Derrick said. "I'll talk to her and see if she can help."

"Let me know if she finds a lead and I'll look into it."

Derrick agreed, and Slade thanked him and headed back to his office.

Nina was waiting when he returned, and she sat quietly as they drove to the hospital. That quiet strength roused his protective instincts.

Worse, her scent, some sweet fruity fragrance, stirred his desires.

But he tamped them down. Nina Nash was a case, nothing more. Slade would never give his heart to a woman. Loving and losing was too damn hard.

First his mother and sister. Then his men… all the people he'd cared about and failed.

He veered into the hospital parking lot and parked, and they walked silently inside. He introduced himself to the receptionist. "Is your hospital administrator in?"

She frowned and checked the schedule. "Dr. Lake has gone home for the day. He'll be in tomorrow at nine."

"How about Dr. Emery?"

She punched in a number, spoke into the phone then turned to them. "He's with a patient, but you can go to his office on the second floor and wait there."

"Thanks." Slade coaxed Nina to the elevator, noting the tense way she held her shoulders. When they passed the nursery, grief and a wistfulness settled in her blue eyes. Newborns filled the bassinets; pink and blue blankets indicating the gender, while a young couple stood goo-goo-eyed, waving at their son through the window.

The intensive-care part of the unit was housed in a separate room beside the regular nursery, and one tiny infant plugged with tubes and wires lay inside an incubator, kicking wildly.

"He's a fighter," Nina said softly as she paused for a moment to watch. "Just like Peyton."

He pressed a hand to her back in comfort, and she stiffened slightly, then inhaled and moved on down the hall to Dr. Emery's office.

Slade surveyed the room as they stepped inside. Medical journals and books overflowed a wall-to-wall bookshelf behind a massive cherry desk that was neat and orderly.

Nina slid into a chair, but Slade stood with his arms folded and studied the man's credentials on the wall between the windows. UNC. Duke. A third wall held a bulletin board decorated with photos of children he'd delivered.

"Is your baby's photo here?" he asked.

Nina's shoulders stiffened as she shook her head. He gritted his teeth, regretting the question. Some people reacted to a person's death as if they'd never existed at all.

A minute later a bushy-haired, freckled man around five-eleven strode in. The moment he saw Nina, a frown swept across his craggy face. "Nina?"

"Yes, Dr. Emery, I'm back." She gestured toward Slade. "This is Slade Blackburn. He's with Guardian Angel Investigations."

Dr. Emery's eyes narrowed, his thick, graying eyebrows crinkling.

"I need to ask you some questions about the night of the hospital fire," Slade said without preamble. "I want to know exactly what happened to Peyton Nash."

NINA TRIED TO STUDY the doctor with an objective eye. But too many times he'd encouraged her to stop asking questions, so many that his dismissal of her had roused her suspicions.

"Honestly, Nina, you've hired another private investigator?" Dr. Emery asked, his tone reeking of exasperation.

"Yes, she has," Slade said. "And I'd like to hear your version of what happened to Peyton."

The doctor fiddled with the stethoscope around his neck, then sank into his office chair as if weary of her. "Nina knows exactly what happened, Mr. Blackburn, but she refuses to accept the truth, that her baby was lost in that fire." His frown accentuated the deep grooves carved by age bracketing his mouth. "It was sad, horrific, tragic," he continued. "But it happened."

Slade simply stared at the man. "According

to Nina, nurses rescued three other infants. Why not her baby?"

"That I don't know," the doctor said. "I spoke with the nurses later, and they all agreed that the baby wasn't in the nursery when the fire broke out, that they thought she had been taken to another area for tests."

"They told me they didn't know where she was," Nina said, contradicting him.

A spark of temper darkened Dr. Emery's eyes. He shuffled a stack of papers on his desk, restacking them in an attempt at stalling. "I didn't want to add to your distress at the time, Nina, but I had ordered heart tests for your infant. I suspected your baby had a hole in her heart as well as underdeveloped lungs, and that she wasn't going to make it."

Nina's breath caught in her throat. "So she might have been somewhere else in the hospital, not in the unit when it burned down."

"We've been over this," Dr. Emery said as if talking to a child. "She did not survive."

"How can you be so sure?" Slade asked. "Did forensics ever prove the infant was in the fire?"

Dr. Emery glared at Slade. "No, but the place, the ashes…it was impossible to identify all the bodies."

"How about security tapes?" Slade asked.

"The explosion knocked them all out." He sighed. "Mr. Blackburn, you're doing Miss Nash an injustice by dredging up the past and raising her hopes. She needs to let her daughter's death go so she can heal."

Slade's jaw clenched. "You tried to persuade Nina to give up her baby for adoption, didn't you?"

The man curled his hand around a stress ball on his desk and squeezed it. "Yes. She was young, unemployed and single."

"But she wanted to keep the baby," Slade said.

"She was immature. And her father didn't intend to support her or the child. I was trying to think of the baby. *If* she made it," he continued, "there would be medical bills, therapy." He shot a condescending look at Nina. "Miss Nash was not equipped to handle those expenses, much less raise a handicapped child."

"That was my problem, not yours," Nina said bitterly.

Dr. Emery pushed away from his desk. "I was, as always, looking out for my patients."

Slade slapped a fist on the desk. "Well, someone didn't look out for Peyton Nash that night, did they?"

Dr. Emery paced to the window, agitated.

"You have no idea how traumatic it was. The hospital staff did everything possible to save the patients."

Slade folded his arms. "And maybe you saw that chaos as an opportunity to take Peyton, to give her to someone else you deemed as a more appropriate parent. Or hell, maybe you sold her for the money."

Hot fury heated the doctor's cheeks. "How dare you imply such slander. I have an impeccable reputation. And I've lived and worked here in Sanctuary all my life."

Slade stood, towering over him. "I don't like the fact that you've stonewalled my client and dismissed her questions without adequately responding."

"I have answered them, but Nina is obsessive and delusional," Emery argued.

Nina flinched, but Slade continued, his voice cold and harsh, "I don't think so. And I don't intend to accept anything you say at face value or leave this case alone, not until all of our questions are answered to my satisfaction." He gestured to Nina. "And if I find out that you withheld information or that you've been lying, I'll be back, and I will hold you responsible."

Fear flashed in the doctor's eyes for the first time since Nina had known him. Was he afraid because Slade was right—did he know something that he wasn't telling them?

SLADE GROUND HIS TEETH as he and Nina left Dr. Emery's office. "Let's see if any of the nurses you mentioned are here."

Nina nodded, and they walked to the nurses' station. "Excuse me," Slade said. "Do you have a nurse named Carrie or Jane working here?"

A middle-aged dirty blonde with green eyes glanced up from the desk. "Yes, Carrie Poole, but she won't be in until tomorrow. And Jane is on vacation and won't be back until next week."

"All right," Slade said. "We'll be back tomorrow."

"What do you think?" Nina asked as they exited the building and walked to his car.

"I don't know yet, Nina," Slade said. "I don't like Emery, but that doesn't necessarily mean he's lying."

Nina's shoulders sagged, and he pressed a hand to her waist to help her in the car.

"But I meant what I said. I will find the answers." He offered her a sad smile. "I just hope the answers are what you want to hear. But I won't lie to you or B.S. you either."

"Thank you," Nina said, her eyes sincere.

"I know some people think I'm unstable, but I'm not. I just have to know the truth."

He stared at her for a long moment, grateful to hear the strength beneath the fragile-looking exterior. He had a feeling Nina Nash was a lot tougher than anyone had given her credit for.

Moonlight flickered off her creamy skin and highlighted her golden hair, and a surge of sexual attraction shot through him.

Damn. Not good.

Determined to avoid personal involvement, he jerked his eyes away from her, started the engine and drove back to GAI headquarters.

He parked and told Nina he'd call her in the morning. A storm cloud rumbled, threatening rain, and she thanked him again and climbed from the car.

"Get some sleep," he called just before she turned away.

But her distressed look indicated that she didn't expect to rest, that dreams of her daughter haunted her nights.

Slade had his own share of nightmares, and as much as he'd like to comfort her, he wasn't a hero. The men he'd lost were.

But he would investigate.

Tomorrow he'd ask Gage and Amanda to pull all the police and medical reports from the hospital. Maybe Amanda could use her expertise to determine if Peyton Nash's body had been among those in the fire.

NINA'S PHONE WAS RINGING as she let herself into her house. Thinking it might be Slade, she hurried to answer it.

But the voice on the other end of the line startled her. William.

"Nina, what the hell are you doing hiring a private investigator?"

Nina tensed at the rage in his tone. "How do you know I hired a P.I.?"

"Dr. Emery called. He's worried that you're having another breakdown."

Nina gripped the phone tighter. "Well, I'm not. And what I do is none of your business, William. You gave up that right the day you walked out on me and our baby."

"Listen to me, Nina. I don't need some nosy P.I. in my business, especially asking questions about something that happened years ago."

"*Something* that happened?" Nina said, her own fury mounting. "What happened was that your daughter went missing. That I was told she died, but that no one ever proved it or even bothered to look for her."

"For God's sake, you need psychiatric help,"

William bellowed. "My mother tried to warn me, but I thought eventually you'd come to your senses."

"Maybe you don't want me asking questions because you have something to hide," Nina said between clenched teeth.

William's breath wheezed with anger. "If you make trouble for me, Nina, I'll make sure everyone at the school where you teach knows just what a basket case you are. Do you think the people of Sanctuary will want an obsessive nutcase teaching their precious children?"

Adrenaline sizzled through Nina's blood. "Are you threatening me, William?"

"Take it however you want, Nina, just leave me alone and tell that P.I. to do the same."

Nina started to shout at him, but he slammed down the phone, cutting her off.

She stared at the dead phone in her hand, then dropped it into its cradle, paced to the mantel and picked up Peyton's photo. "I won't give up," she whispered. "Not even if William did threaten me."

In spite of her resolve not to do it, she walked into the bedroom, dragged on her nightshirt then slipped open the drawer where she'd stowed the tiny pink dress with the butterflies on it that she'd bought years ago.

The outfit she'd planned for Peyton to wear home. She knew it was crazy to have kept it. Pathetic.

But she crawled in bed, pressed it to her chest and inhaled the sweet scent of fabric softener.

Then she closed her eyes and imagined her daughter coming home.

Eight-year-old Rebecca Davis fumbled for her glasses, sweeping her hand across the desk in the bedroom at her foster parents' house. Without the glasses, she was nearly blind. But at least the social worker had gotten her a computer with big print.

She hated the clunky glasses though. They were too big for her face, and some of the kids teased her and called her *Four Eyes*.

Other kids looked at her with pity just because she was handicapped, and she didn't have a mommy.

She didn't want them to feel sorry for her. She did want a mommy though.

She clicked on the keyboard, brought up her journal and began to type.

Mommy, I know you're out there somewhere. I prayed that you would find me on

Mother's Day but that's passed, so maybe you will on my birthday.

I don't like it here. The house is dark and dusty. And Mama Reese says her knees hurt too much to play with me outside. Papa Reese's cigarettes make my eyes itchy and watery and then I cough, and then he tells me to shut up. They don't like my singing either.

I have to sing though. I dream sometimes that you're looking for me. That you didn't just leave me. That we just got losted from each other, and that you can hear me. That one day you'll follow my voice and come and get me.

She swiped at a tear running down her cheek. Crying was for babies but sometimes she couldn't help it. Sniffling and swallowing to hold back more tears, she finished the journal entry.

I know I look kind of dorky, and I'm little for my age, and I can't run like the other kids. And one of my eyes looks funny because I can't see out of it, but I take my medicine every day so I don't have the seizures anymore.

I'm getting better in school, too. I'm only

a year behind. I've been practicing my writing, and I can almost make the letters right now. I can pour my own cereal and make my own peanut butter and jelly sandwiches. And I don't mind wearing hand-me-downs if you don't have much money.

Please come and get me, Mommy. I promise not to be any trouble.

She saved her entry, then pulled on her pj's and crawled in bed. Then she closed her eyes and prayed her mommy would hear her this time and come to get her as she began to sing....

Chapter Four

Slade let himself into the fixer-upper house he'd purchased on the side of the mountain. The wooden two-story needed painting, a new roof, the wood floors needed to be stripped and restained and boards needed replacing on the wraparound porch.

He'd thought doing the work himself would be cathartic, but he'd yet to change a thing. Still, the place had character and at one time was probably a cozy home for some family.

He scoffed. As a kid, he'd dreamed about having a home like this. Now it didn't seem to matter.

But the place was isolated and offered him privacy, as well as an abundance of wide-open mountain air. Something he'd desperately needed after Iraq and the place he'd been kept when he'd been taken prisoner. Cramped, dark, filthy, bug-infested, the stench, the human wastes…

And the blood from the soldiers who'd died trying to save him.

He inhaled a deep, calming breath, the summer air filling his nostrils with the scent of honeysuckle and wildflowers, chasing away the demons from his past. He had a job to do now, and he'd focus on that. Get through the day.

One hour at a time.

He spotted the bottle of whiskey on the counter, and the temptation to reach for it, to pour himself a mind-numbing shot seized him. Just one drink to erase the images in his head.

No… He was done burying his pain. He'd have to learn to live with it or it would destroy him. Then he couldn't atone for his sins.

Instead, he strode to the workout room he'd created off the garage, yanked on boxing gloves and began to pound his punching bag. The faces of his bleeding and dying men haunted him, and he hit the bag harder, the rage eating his soul, chipping away at his sanity.

He had to learn to control it. Focus. Forget.

No, he couldn't forget. Forgetting would mean dishonoring the sacrifices they'd made.

He wished to hell they'd just left him to die and saved themselves.

And their wives and families...three wives left alone now because of him.

His sister dead.

His mother gone.

He'd failed them all.

He would not fail Nina Nash.

Her story echoed in his head as he punched and slammed his fists into the bag, over and over, venting his anger over his own past and the anguish he'd heard in her voice.

But you might fail her, a voice taunted. *You might because she wants you to find her daughter alive.*

And you might discover she really is dead.

He slammed the bag so hard it swung back wildly, then came toward him and he punched it again. Again and again and again until sweat poured down his back and face, until his body ached and blood oozed from beneath the gloves.

Finally, when he'd purged his anger, he ripped off the gloves, went to the bathroom, showered then booted up his computer. He nuked a slice of leftover pizza and wolfed it down with a bottle of vitamin water while he searched news reports regarding infants' and children's deaths reported during the past eight years.

He specifically searched for any cases regarding premature births or babies found dead following the hospital fire.

Three different cases caught his eye, one baby who'd been found in a Dumpster two weeks to the day after Peyton had gone missing.

NINA JERKED AWAKE, the sound of the little girl's singing echoing in her head.

The angelic voice… A song from *Mary Poppins*…

It had to belong to her daughter.

Or was she imagining it as the therapist had said? Creating a voice that she thought her daughter might sound like and playing it in her head because she couldn't bear to let her go?

She closed her eyes and burrowed beneath the quilt, willing herself to fall back asleep so she could hear the voice again. Sometimes, the little voice sounded so close that it seemed the child was in the room with her. Sometimes, she knew that if she slept long enough, she would see her face in her dreams, that maybe Peyton could tell her where she was so she could find her.

Instead of the beautiful little girl's song though, William's threat reverberated in her head. Dr. Emery had wasted no time in calling him. He'd probably phoned her father, as well.

They'd probably all sighed and made sympathetic noises and lamented over her mental state. For all she knew, they were planning another intervention to convince her to check herself back into the loony bin.

She would not go back there. She wasn't crazy or demented.

She was simply a mother who needed to find her child.

A noise startled her, and she clenched the covers, certain she'd heard someone outside. The wind whistled, a tree limb scraped her window and an animal howled somewhere in the distance.

She sighed, willing herself to calm down.

She couldn't lapse into paranoia again, not the way she had after she'd lost Peyton.

But another noise, a creaking sound on the front porch, sent her vaulting up from bed. Outside, thunder rumbled, and the trees shook violently, the sound of rain splattering the windowpanes, making a staticky sound like drums beating in the night.

She grabbed her robe, tied it around her

waist and tiptoed to the den, shivering as the air conditioner kicked on. Darkness bathed the room, but a streak of lightning flashed in a jagged line and she froze, her heart pounding.

Had she seen someone on her porch? The silhouette of a shadow?

Fear surged through her, and she reached for the phone.

But the times when she'd called the sheriff flashed back. The way he'd dismissed her fears and ordered her to get some help, then claimed she was inventing shadows in the night.

His calls to her father…the never-ending cycle of his disdainful looks…

She dropped the phone in its cradle, grabbed the umbrella from the stand by the door then slipped the edge of the curtain sheer aside and searched the darkness.

Rain pounded the roof and porch, running in rivulets down the sides of the awning, and down the street a car's lights floated through the fog, disappearing into the blur.

The streetlight in the cul-de-sac on the other end of the street illuminated wet pavement and another house but its lights were off.

Holding her breath, she listened for signs

of someone outside, but the storm raged on, the sound of a cat screeching echoing above the rain. Her heart squeezed, and she slowly unlocked the door.

Keeping the umbrella poised in case someone had been on the porch, she pulled the door ajar and the dripping cat darted down the steps.

Then her eyes widened and a sob gurgled in her throat.

God, no...

A small rag doll lay on the porch in front of the door, a knife sticking through its heart.

A doll just like the one she'd found right before she'd had her breakdown, a doll her father and the psychiatrist had insisted she'd put there as some sort of manifestation of her grief and guilt.

SLADE RARELY SLEPT and this night was no different. When he did, the nightmares came.

He'd choose fatigue over the memories haunting him any day.

Antsy to get started, he brewed a pot of coffee and was at the phone by six.

The reporter, a guy named Hewey Darby, had quoted a Detective Swarnson from the neighboring county as the lead detective on the Dumpster case, so he punched in his number, anxious to hear what the man had to say.

When the receptionist for the police department answered, he asked to speak to Swarnson. "I'm sorry, sir, but Detective Swarnson is no longer with us."

"Where can I get in touch with him?"

A moment of hesitation. "I'm afraid you can't. He was killed last year in a random shooting. What is this about?"

He explained that he wanted information on the Dumpster-baby case. "Oh, then you can speak with his partner, Detective Little. I'll connect you to her office."

"Thank you."

A minute later, a woman's voice echoed back. "Detective Little."

"This is Slade Blackburn, Guardian Angel Investigations. I'm investigating the case of an infant who went missing eight years ago in Sanctuary, the same night as the deadly fire and explosion that caused numerous deaths."

"Right. I read about the arrests."

"One of the patients in the hospital at the time was told that her baby died, but her body was never recovered, so I'm investigating the possibility that the child might have been kidnapped."

"I'm not sure how I can help."

"Actually, I'm not sure you can either, but I'm exploring every possible lead. I found records of a case you and your partner investigated where an infant was found in a Dumpster approximately two weeks after the child in question went missing."

"Oh, right, I remember that case."

"What can you tell me about it? Did you ID the child?"

"As a matter of fact, we did." Her voice warbled. "The mother was a crack addict. She delivered early, but the child wasn't breathing so she freaked out and decided to get rid of it for fear she'd be caught."

"Did you arrest her?"

"She's in prison now." A long sigh. "I'm sorry. I guess that's not much help."

"No, it means that the child I'm looking for might be alive."

"If it's been eight years…" Detective Little said. "You know the chances are slim that you'll find her."

Slade gritted his teeth. "I know. But everyone assumed she died in that fire. The fact that there was no body or proof means there might have been foul play."

"Good luck, Mr. Blackburn. I have a soft spot for kids myself, that's why I work Special Victims. If I can help you any other way, just let me know."

He thanked her, then spent the next hour chasing down the other two instances he'd read about, but both turned out to be dead ends, too.

The rain died, the morning sun fighting through the storm clouds. His phone buzzed, and he checked the number. Nina.

He punched the connect button. "Nina?"

"Slade...can you come over?"

"What's wrong?"

"Someone left a rag doll with a knife in its heart on my doorstep."

Slade cursed, grabbed his weapon, shoved it in his holster, threw on a jacket and rushed outside.

Nina's hand trembled as she hung up the phone. Nausea rolled through her as she stared at the doll, and her chest ached so badly it was as if that knife had been plunged into her own heart.

Someone had put the doll on her doorstep to taunt her with the past.

Who would be so cruel?

She rushed upstairs and threw on some

clothes, then made coffee and tried to sip it while she waited.

Five minutes later, Slade's SUV rumbled up the drive and she inhaled deeply. She had to pull herself together. She finally had someone on her side, and she couldn't chance losing his services now.

Brushing her hair back into a ponytail, she rushed to the door. The sight of Slade Blackburn on her front porch sent a surge of relief through her.

The wind tousled his hair around his broad face, and the trees shook raindrops from the branches, scattering them across the ground. "Are you all right?" he asked.

She nodded. "Yes, just shaken."

"Tell me what happened."

"Before dawn, I heard a noise outside." She led him to the sofa table. Her hand shook as she picked up the doll. "Then I found this on my porch."

His eyes flashed with anger. "Damn sicko. Did you see who put it on your porch?"

"No, but I saw a shadow outside. Then I heard a car leaving down the street."

Slade's jaw tightened. "Do you have a bag I can put it in? I'll send it to the lab for prints and DNA."

"Sure." She rushed to the kitchen and

returned with one, and he used his handkerchief to seal it in the bag.

The temptation to share what happened in the past taunted her, but she decided to hold off.

Maybe he'd find a lead from the doll and she wouldn't have to divulge the humiliating details of her breakdown.

Chapter Five

Slade gritted his teeth. Nina looked shaken, fragile and exhausted, like a delicate flower that had been crushed in the wind.

But dammit, she also looked beautiful in that pale blue cotton blouse and that flowing black shirt. He itched to pull her into his arms and comfort her but gripped his hands by his sides to keep from touching her.

Someone, whoever had put that doll on her porch, had meant to torment her.

Or maybe the doll had been left as a warning. If she kept asking questions, the same thing would happen to her…

Hopefully Amanda could lift some prints. If not, she might be able to track down where the doll and knife were bought and the buyer.

Slade gritted his teeth. The fact that she'd received it the day after she'd hired him was significant.

Dammit, he didn't like the fact that someone was watching her. Someone who obviously didn't want her asking questions. That fact alone roused his suspicions and gave credence to her case.

The first suspect who came to mind was the doctor. But surely the man was too smart to pull such a stunt. He'd have to know that he would be the first person Slade would question.

"Other than Dr. Emery, who else knows that you hired me?" Slade asked.

Nina ran a hand over her forehead. "William."

His gaze shot to hers. "Peyton's father?"

She nodded and folded her arms across her chest. "He phoned last night."

Slade growled, "How did he find out?"

"Dr. Emery called him."

"Son of a bitch."

Nina's gaze jerked to his, and he forced himself to tamp his anger. "What did he say?"

"He was upset," Nina said. "William doesn't want anyone messing up his life by dredging up his past. Especially me."

Slade frowned. "I don't give a damn what he wants. He's going to talk to me. And I'll get the truth out of him one way or another."

NINA'S HEART WARMED. For the first time in eight years, she actually felt as if someone believed her.

That someone else might care that her daughter had gone missing, when her father and Peyton's own father had accepted her disappearance as if it had been a blessing in disguise.

"Do you want me to call William and tell him we're coming?" Nina asked.

"No, I want the element of surprise on our side when I confront him."

Our side? A warmth spread through Nina at the thought of this man defending her. For so long, she felt as if she'd been waging an uphill battle all alone.

The sun glinted through the clouds, the traffic thick as they left the mountain roads and turned onto the highway toward Winston-Salem. The interstate buzzed with early-morning traffic and commuters.

"Did you grow up in Sanctuary?" Slade asked.

"No, in Raleigh. I attended a private school. That's where I met William. His father lived there before opening a practice in Winston-Salem."

"So how did you end up in Sanctuary?"

Nina sighed. "When I got pregnant, my

father rented a small house in town. He wanted to hide me away from the people he knew in Raleigh, especially his business colleagues. I stayed in the house until after Peyton was born, then Daddy wanted me to come back and live with him, but I…couldn't."

Slade's thick, dark brows furrowed. "Let me get this straight. He moved you to a different town and left you alone when you were pregnant and just a teenager?"

Nina shrugged at the censure in his voice. "It was better that way. We weren't exactly getting along back then." She stroked the sides of her arms with her hands, shaking off the memories. "What about you? Where are you from?"

Slade's jaw tightened. "All around. My dad was in the military. He died in combat."

Nina wanted to soothe the anguish she heard beneath his calm veneer but sensed he wouldn't welcome her touch, so she held herself back. "I'm sorry, Slade. How old were you?"

He maneuvered around an eighteen-wheeler. "Thirteen."

"I'm sure that was difficult on everyone."

He made a grunting sound. "Yeah. Two years later my sister disappeared, and my mother totally lost it."

Just as she had when Peyton first went missing.

But she hadn't abandoned a second child who needed her. "And they left you to fend for yourself," Nina said softly.

Slade stiffened. "I was the man of the family," he said. "I was supposed to take care of them and I failed."

"Slade…"

"Drop it, Nina." His expression warned her not to push. "Where does William live?"

"Downtown. He bought a half-million-dollar condo directly across the street from his law office."

"He must be doing well."

"Yes. Losing Peyton wasn't even a blip on the radar for him," she said, fighting bitterness.

He found a parking spot, parked and they climbed out and walked over to the condo complex. People clogged the sidewalk, walking to work; the coffee shop was overflowing with early-morning patrons and horns and traffic noises filled the air.

They stepped into the entryway of the high-rise building, then stopped at the front desk to speak to security. "We're here to see William Hood."

A middle-aged dark-haired woman greeted them. "Is Mr. Hood expecting you?"

"No," Slade said. "But it's important."

Nina cleared her throat. "Just tell him that Nina Nash needs to see him."

The woman buzzed his condo, announced their arrival then spoke quietly into the headset. A second later, she turned back to them with a frown. "I'm sorry, but he says he doesn't want to see you."

Slade slapped his hand on the counter. "Tell him he can talk to us now or we'll be waiting at his office."

The woman's brows rose, then she spoke into the headset again. This time curiosity lined her face when she glanced back up. "He's in the penthouse."

Slade harrumphed. "Of course."

The woman frowned again as they made their way to the elevator. Nina's stomach thrashed as the elevator carried them up, her ears popping as they climbed to the twenty-ninth floor. The doors finally swished open, and she swayed slightly. Silently Slade took her elbow and guided her to the door, then punched the doorbell.

A snarling William opened the door dressed in a three-piece suit, his sandy-blond hair combed back from his forehead and set with gel, his blue eyes like ice chips. Looking at him compared to Slade made her wonder why she'd been stupid enough to give him her virginity.

"Nina, what in the hell do you think you're doing?" William barked. "Didn't you understand my warning last night?"

"Warning?" Slade asked in a lethal tone.

Nina shifted. "William threatened to tell my coworkers at school that I'm crazy."

"Is that so?" Slade glared at William. "Well, I'm working for Nina now, Hood, and I don't like bullies."

A vein throbbed in William's forehead. "And I don't like smarmy P.I.'s nosing into my business."

A nasty grin slid onto Slade's face. "You don't, huh? Well, you'd better get used to it, because I'm just getting started." He shouldered his way past William into the foyer of the condo. "And no one, especially some skinny-assed lawyer, is going to stop me."

SLADE GROUND HIS TEETH in an attempt to rein in his temper. He couldn't tolerate any man who'd abandon his own child, and this man had rejected his before his baby had even been born.

To think that Hood would use his money, status and weight to intimidate Nina infuriated him.

If it were his own child and he were in Nina's situation, he'd move hell and high water to find out the truth, just as she was.

"Mister—"

"Blackburn," Slade cut in.

"Either leave or I'm going to call security."

"William, please," Nina interjected. "All we want is a few minutes."

William gave her a seething look. "There's nothing to talk about, Nina. We've been over this a thousand times."

"You never wanted to have a child, did you?" Slade asked.

William glared at him but drew a breath, adopting a professional mask that Slade was sure he used in court. Probably to free any low-life slimeball who paid his salary.

And judging from the condo and the pricey modern furnishings, he either had a lot of clients or his fees were enormous.

Hood checked his Rolex. "Excuse me now, I have work to do."

Slade caught his arm. "First you're going to answer some questions."

Hood jerked free of Slade, his suit jacket crinkling as he squared his shoulders. Finally he gave a labored sigh. "Five minutes."

The temptation to hit the bastard was so strong, Slade rolled his hands into fists. "What makes you so sure that your baby died in the fire in Sanctuary?"

A cold look settled in Hood's eyes. "If you'd seen that explosion, the chaos, the debris… you'd know there's no way that anyone left inside survived." He paused. "And Nina and the sheriff certainly questioned everyone at the hospital."

"Maybe not," Slade said. "You're a lawyer. Kidnappings happen in hospitals all the time. Can you honestly say that it wasn't possible for someone to have carried your baby outside and disappeared with her?"

For the briefest of moments, Slade saw Hood's mind working, saw the hesitation in his eyes, a moment where he actually considered the possibility. But it quickly disappeared, and the uncaring façade returned, his skepticism firmly tucked in place.

"Even if it were possible, it didn't happen," Hood said. "According to the police, every other baby was accounted for. The unit exploded before the rescue workers could save Nina's child."

"She was your child, too," Slade pointed out.

Beside him, he felt Nina's wave of pain as if it had washed through him. But she didn't react. In fact, he admired the way she maintained her composure.

"Nina and I came to an agreement before the child was born," Hood said sharply.

Slade gave a sarcastic laugh. "You came to an agreement? You mean you acted like a spoiled, selfish prick and declared that you didn't want the child."

"I was only nineteen," Hood said defensively. "I had plans."

Nina folded her arms. "So did I. But that didn't mean that I could walk away from our baby."

"That's right, Nina. You're such a damn saint," Hood bit out. "You can't even let the child go when everyone has told you she's dead."

A brunette with wavy hair and catlike eyes appeared with a frown, her silk pantsuit flowing freely. "What's going on, honey?"

Hood jerked his head toward her. "Mitzi, we have company," Hood said. "Nina and her new detective, Mr. Blackburn."

"God, Nina," the woman muttered. "Don't tell me you're nagging William again."

Hood wrapped his arm around Mitzi's shoulders. "Sorry, sweetheart, but she's still as crazy as ever."

"We were discussing the night of the fire in Sanctuary," Slade cut in. "You seem certain of the facts, Hood, but I spoke with Dr. Emery, the ob-gyn, and I think the case is worth investigating."

Slade removed the bagged doll from inside his jacket and held it up. "In fact, last night someone left this on Nina's doorstep."

Mitzi made a shocked sound, then clung to William's arm as if she feared Slade had stabbed the doll himself just for effect.

Slade directed his comment to Hood. "Where were you last night?"

Mitzi answered before Hood could respond. "He was with me. All night," she said with a suggestive smile.

Hood made a clicking sound with his teeth. "Blackburn, you poor, dumb sucker. Obviously Nina forgot to mention a few details about her past."

"William, don't," Nina said in a choked whisper.

"Don't what, Nina?" Hood scowled at her.

"Tell him the truth, that you've pulled this same stunt before?"

Slade shot Hood an angry look, but something about the guilt in Nina's eyes warned him to tread slowly. He was here to investigate, find out the truth, whether or not Nina liked it.

Whether or not he did.

"What are you talking about?" Slade asked.

William's expression turned pitying. "Nina has a habit of suckering people in with her sweet smile and big, sad eyes. But she's unstable. She has been for a long time."

"If you're referring to the fact that she had a breakdown after her baby went missing, then yes. I am aware of that."

Hood arched a brow. "So she explained the details of her psychosis?"

Guilt and worry slashed her face. "William, don't—"

The look Nina exchanged with Hood made apprehension knot Slade's belly. He'd insisted Nina be honest with him, but apparently she hadn't shared everything.

"After Nina lost the baby, she did things like this. She bought a rag doll like this one, then claimed that someone stuck a knife in its heart and left it on her doorstep."

Slade stood ramrod still, forcing himself not to react.

Hood continued, "She also said that she packed up the baby things and stored them in the attic, but then insisted she came home one night and found them scattered across her bedroom."

"I didn't scatter those baby things around," Nina argued. "They were packed away in my closet."

"That's not what the psychiatrist reported," William said, then turned back to Slade. "Nina also swore that someone put a CD of lullabies in her car and that sometimes she'd wake up at night and one would be playing but that she hadn't started it."

Nina started to speak, but Hood was on a roll and sneered down at her. "Oh, and did she tell you about the voices? She swears she hears her little girl singing to her at night. A *Mary Poppins* song, right, Nina?"

"Stop it!" Nina turned and ran from the condo, her sob echoing in the air behind her.

Slade didn't know what to believe. But he didn't like Hood and refused to let him bait him, so he gave him a steely look. "If I discover you had anything to do with your child's disappearance or those things happening to

Nina, you'll pay." He jabbed a finger at Hood's chest. "And no amount of money will save you."

NINA SLAMMED THE SUV door, and leaned her head into her hands. This couldn't be happening again.

Yes, she heard the voices. Her daughter singing. But that was *real*.

Only everyone had made her doubt herself. And then all those creepy things had started happening…and she'd finally broken down.

Heat warmed her cheeks, and she suddenly felt nauseated. The sound of the driver's door opening rent the air, and Slade's masculine scent filled the close confines. This morning she'd felt as if she might have found an ally. Maybe even a friend.

But his anger permeated the tension-filled air as he climbed inside, and she found she'd lost that ally now.

God help her. She had to make him believe her. "Slade—"

He threw up a hand, silently ordering her not to speak. "I warned you yesterday when I took this case that you had to be honest with me."

"But—"

"Stop, Nina," Slade said in a harsh voice.

"Don't lie to me now or ever again." He started the engine. "I'm going to talk to your father, and if I discover that you made up the story about this doll to get attention, we're finished."

Chapter Six

Hurt knifed through Nina, and she folded her arms and stared out the window as Slade drove toward Raleigh.

Her father would probably verify William's story, paint her as a sad, demented freak just as William had.

She should be used to people's reactions to her breakdown, but she didn't know if she'd ever totally become immune.

She had not stabbed the doll and put it on her porch the night before, just as she hadn't years ago. She also hadn't strewn baby paraphernalia all over the house or put those CDs in her car and house.

Not that she remembered anyway…

No. She wasn't going to doubt herself again. The doctors and therapists had almost convinced her that she was delusional with grief and stress and the effects of the antidepressants. But she wasn't taking antidepressants now, and she had recovered from the breakdown.

Not to mention that the person tormenting her had driven her over the edge.

And now the taunts were starting all over...

Because she'd hired a private investigator.

Couldn't Slade see that that meant someone didn't want her learning the truth?

She opened her mouth to argue, but quickly clamped it shut. Hadn't she learned from experience that protesting and trying to explain only made things worse? Made her sound more pathetic and desperate?

She hated to look pathetic in his eyes.

But how could she explain the voices she heard at night? The little girl's voice singing to her? The sense that she was singing so Nina would come for her...

The words to the song, her soft soprano voice, was like an angel's, the voice mesmerizing her just as the Pied Piper's flute had enthralled the children.

The silence became painful during the drive, Slade's withdrawal hurting more than she could imagine.

"Tell me about Mitzi," he finally said quietly.

Embarrassment heated her cheeks. Mitzi

had married William…and made a fool of her.

She licked her dry lips and sucked up her pride. If she wanted his help, and she *did,* she had to be honest. Pride be damned.

"She was Miss Popular in high school and came from a prestigious family. Her father worked abroad so she traveled and studied in prep schools all over the world before they moved back to Raleigh her senior year."

"She seemed to be jealous of you," Slade commented.

Nina gave a sardonic little laugh. "Jealous? Why would she be jealous of me?"

"Because you slept with William and had his baby."

Nina chewed her bottom lip. "*Jealousy* isn't the word I'd use. She hated me."

Memories flooded her. "Mitzi was one of the *it* girls. Plastic, if you know what I mean. She served on every school committee, led the dance squad and was voted prom queen." She sighed. "All the boys wanted Mitzi."

"And Mitzi?"

"She wanted William." Nina picked at a piece of lint on her shirt. It was so long ago, it shouldn't still hurt. But she'd been young and foolish and naive.

"So you fought over him?'"

Nina laughed. "Not really. In fact, William never showed any interest in me until after Mitzi broke up with him."

"*She* broke up with *him?*"

"They had some kind of stupid fight a week before prom, and so he asked me. I realize now he only wanted to get back at her."

She felt his eyes boring into her face, but she couldn't quite look at him. "It's really such a cliché. Shy girl goes to prom with the big guy on campus. Gets pregnant. He goes back to the girl he really loves."

Slade muttered an obscenity. "But Mitzi didn't take the pregnancy so well?"

She laughed again. It was either laugh or cry. And she would never cry again over Mitzi or William Hood. "No. She spread the word at school that I was a whore. That I'd thrown myself at William and promised him sex if he'd take me to the prom."

In spite of her resolve to overcome the bitterness, it resonated in her voice. "That's when my father moved me out of town."

Another dark, seething look passed over his face, settling into his deep brown eyes. Eyes that looked permanently angry at the world.

And now angry at her.

She stiffened her spine. She didn't give a

damn if he was angry with her or not. She'd hired him to do a job.

And she'd put up with anything he threw at her, even his ridicule, his pity, his disbelief, as long as he followed through.

Finding out the truth about Peyton was the only thing that mattered.

SLADE CONTEMPLATED WHAT he'd learned about Nina, William Hood and his wife, as they wound up the mile-long drive to Nina's father's estate.

Hood was a first-class bastard, his wife a major bitch.

But that didn't necessarily mean they were lying, just that they'd been young, selfish, immature and relieved to be free of an unwanted child.

He tried to put himself in their places, but empathy wasn't his style, not for spoiled rich kids whose priorities were majorly skewed.

And not when they were so callous toward an innocent baby.

Especially Hood, who'd shared the child's blood.

Slade surveyed Nash's house as he pulled in front of the circular drive. Pristine gardens, sculpted bushes, ornately carved molding and granite lion statues adorned the front of the

mansion, a massive white antebellum repro-
duction set in the midst of ancient oaks and a
pond complete with ducks, as well as a massive outdoor patio obviously designed for
entertaining.

"Your father must be doing quite well."

"I suppose," Nina said in an oddly distant
voice.

"You don't know?"

"He's in banking, finance, stocks. He did
well in the past, but I haven't kept up with him
in a few years."

He narrowed his eyes. "You don't see each
other regularly?"

A sad look flickered in her eyes. "No.
As a matter of fact, we haven't talked in...
months."

Slade's opinion of the man slipped another
notch. "Then he's going to be surprised to see
us," he said.

Nina opened her car door and climbed
out before he could reach it, but the shudder
that coursed up her body confirmed that she
dreaded this confrontation.

After the ordeal with Hood, he understood
her anxiety.

He'd been rough on her in the car, as well.
But dammit, he didn't want to be made a fool
of or go on a wild chase.

Instincts urged him to pursue the case anyway, to find out the truth for Nina once and for all.

Then he could walk away with a clear conscience.

NINA WILLED HERSELF to be strong as they walked up the immaculate drive to the steps to her father's house. This place had never been her home.

Her home was the bungalow in Sanctuary where she'd hoped to raise her little girl.

Slade punched the doorbell, and she breathed deeply, desperately relying on the relaxation exercises she'd learned in therapy. But her palms were sweating, her heart racing, painful memories assaulting her like a knife digging into her heart.

Just like the knife in the doll's chest...

The door opened, and Miss Mosey, the housekeeper her father had kept for the past twelve years, looked shocked as she spotted Nina.

"Miss Nash, we...had no idea you were coming."

"I know, Miss Mosey," Nina said softly. "Is Father here?"

The woman's brows pinched together. Nina had once had affection for the older woman, and thought she might be an ally when she'd discovered her pregnancy, but her father's money had obviously meant more to her than Nina's feelings.

"I'm afraid he just left for the office. He had a luncheon at two and wanted to tie up some things there first."

"Thanks," Nina said. "We'll stop there then." She started to turn to leave, then paused and touched the woman's hand. One of her therapists had suggested that forgiveness would help her heal. "It's good to see you again. I hope you're doing well."

Tears suddenly glittered in the woman's eyes, and she surprised Nina by pulling her into a hug. "I hope you are, too, dear. You and your father should make peace. He misses you so much."

Nina's pulse stuttered, and she hugged the woman back then turned to leave, unable to speak.

By rote, she recited directions to her father's office, contemplating Miss Mosey's comment as Slade crossed traffic into town. Did her father really miss her? If so, why hadn't he tried to contact her?

Slade turned onto Glenwood Avenue, then located Nash's office, a two-story brick building in the heart of the downtown area. He parked in the adjacent parking lot, and they walked to the entrance in silence. Her father hated to be interrupted during business, and Nina considered turning around, but Slade took her arm as if he sensed her anxiety and they went inside the building.

A pretty red-haired receptionist wearing a short, black pencil skirt greeted them from the counter where she was pouring coffee. "Can I help you?"

"Yes, I'm Nina Nash. I'm here to see my father."

"Oh, you're Mr. Nash's daughter," the young woman said with a startled look. "I'm Rochelle. It's nice to meet you. I'll tell him you're here."

Nina wondered faintly if her father was sleeping with the young woman but dismissed the thought. She didn't really care about his personal life. He'd dated dozens of women since her mother's death, but never committed to anyone.

Nina watched Rochelle disappear up the steps with the coffee, her long legs stretching beneath the skirt. A minute later, she returned with a wary smile. "He says to go on up."

Slade placed his hand on the small of her back as she climbed the steps, but her stomach fluttered with nerves. Her father's diplomas, photos of business acquaintances and news-paper clippings about his deals lined the walls.

The door stood ajar, and Nina squared her shoulders, determined not to crumble in front of her father no matter how he reacted to her visit.

SLADE IMMEDIATELY SIZED up Mr. Nash from the edge of his office doorway. A compul-sive, anal workaholic. His office was neat and orderly, dominated by a walnut desk and credenza with a stocked bar at one end. Dark leather furniture created a seating arrange-ment around a fireplace near the bar. Books on finance and business filled a bookshelf on the opposite wall. And Nash was dressed in a three-piece suit that probably cost more than Slade's monthly salary.

The man was lean and tall with light brown hair, an angular face and hands that had prob-ably never touched dirt in his life. He looked cool and focused.

Except for the slight hint of emotion that flickered in his eyes the moment he saw Nina.

"Daddy?" Nina said softly.

"Nina." He hesitated, his voice cracking slightly. "This is a surprise."

"I know," she said, then glanced quickly at him. "Can we come in?"

"Of course." Nash gestured toward the seating area, and Slade followed Nina over to the love seat, where she sat down.

"Mr. Nash, my name is Slade Blackburn. I'm with Guardian Angel Investigations."

"I know who you are." Disdain edged Nash's voice, then he turned toward Nina and sympathy softened his expression. "Dr. Emery phoned to tell me you hired another private investigator, Nina."

Nina clasped her trembling hands in her lap. "Yes. I assume you read the papers and know that GAI discovered that the hospital fire and explosion weren't accidental."

Nash gestured to the bar in offering, but Slade shook his head, declining his silent offer of a drink. Still, Nash removed a bottle of water from a small stainless-steel refrigerator and pushed it into Nina's hands. "Yes, I heard the news. But I don't see what that has to do with you."

Nina stiffened but accepted the water bottle and set it on the table. "They uncovered new evidence, proving people were wrong about how the fire started. That means they might be able to find new evidence about Peyton."

"God, Nina." Nash scrubbed a hand over

the back of his neck. "You have your teaching degree, a job now. I thought you were finally moving on."

"I've tried," Nina said. "But if there's a chance that the police missed something, I have to at least look into it."

Nash angled his head toward Slade. "I don't know how much my daughter shared with you, Mr. Blackburn, but she can't go through this again. The baby didn't survive, end of story. You're wasting your time and giving her false hope if you continue."

Slade chewed the inside of his cheek. "I've reviewed the details of the case, Mr. Nash. Considering the fact that the baby's body was never recovered, and the chaos that night, there is a possibility that someone could have kidnapped the baby." Slade removed the bagged doll and knife.

"And just last night someone left this for Nina. Doesn't it seem coincidental to you that someone would leave this on her porch only hours after she reopened the investigation?"

"Oh, hell." Nash gave Nina a worried look, and paced back to his desk. Frowning, he opened a drawer, removed a folder and walked back toward them. Then he shoved the file toward Slade.

"This is the report from the psychiatrist

who treated Nina after she lost Peyton. Take a look at it and tell me if you really think there's a case here, or if Nina is just unable to accept the truth."

"Dad, you can't show him my medical records." Nina looked appalled. "They're private."

Nina's father stroked her shoulder. "I just don't want to see you put yourself through this kind of pain again." His voice dropped a decibel. "And I certainly don't want you to have another breakdown, Nina. I want to see you happy and building a new life."

Slade's hands tightened around the folder at the sincerity in Nash's voice. For a moment he debated looking at the file, but he'd vowed to find out the truth, and he'd told Nina she had to be completely honest with him.

So he flipped open the folder and skimmed the report. It corroborated Hood's story. According to the psychiatrist's notes, Nina had been in denial, depressed and delusional. The episode with the doll and the knife through its heart symbolized her guilt and grief over not saving her child, and the anguish in her own heart.

Slade's stomach knotted. Had he been a fool to believe her? Was Hood right—had he fallen for her big, anguished eyes because he wanted to be her hero?

A hero for someone because he'd failed time after time after time…

"I AM NOT DELUSIONAL," Nina said emphatically. "Yes, I was grieving, sad, even depressed but not delusional."

"Are you taking antidepressants again?" her father asked.

"No," Nina said. "I didn't want to take them years ago, and I don't intend to ever again." She jutted up her chin, forcing conviction into her voice. "I'm perfectly rational, and I did not stab that doll and put it on my porch. I heard a noise in the night, then got up and saw a shadow outside." Her voice grew stronger. "Don't you care that someone is tormenting me, Dad?"

"This is the way it all started." Her father gave Slade a disgruntled look, then lowered himself into the chair opposite her and pulled her hands into his. "Please go see the therapist again, Nina."

She cast a sideways look at Slade, but his dark eyes probed hers as if she were a bug he was trying to dissect.

Anger fueled her temper. She could handle whatever she discovered about her daughter, but she didn't know if she could tolerate the pitying or condescending looks again. "I should have known that you wouldn't help me, that you wouldn't believe me. You don't want anything to mess up your perfect world, do you, Dad?" She jerked her hands away and stood. "You didn't want a pregnant daughter, or an illegitimate child, and you certainly wouldn't have wanted a preemie who might have been handicapped."

"That's enough, Nina." Her father's eyes glittered with rage. "I love you. Everything I've ever done has been with your best interests in mind."

Nina gripped her shoulder bag, and faced her father. "If you wanted what was best for me, you'd believe me. You would have helped me search for my baby instead of abandoning me and making me feel like I was crazy."

Grief swelled inside her at the realization that she and her father would never get along. Never be close.

She had disappointed him.

But he had disappointed her, too.

He was the one person she'd thought would have had faith in her. But he hadn't trusted in her when she'd needed him most.

She spun around and walked out of the office, knowing she'd never be back.

REBECCA DANGLED HER feet belong the swing, pumping her legs hard to make the swing move back and forth. She was too short to touch the ground, and her legs were weak so it took a bunch of tries, but finally the swing moved.

She didn't care if the kids laughed at her.

She would learn to pump herself even if they teased her until school was out. When her mommy came to get her, she was going to show her everything she'd learned.

A black car drove by the fence near the parking lot, and someone rolled down the window. The sun nearly blinded her, and she scrunched her nose, her glasses slipping down.

But someone in the car pushed a camera out the window and began to snap pictures.

Her stomach spasmed. Why were strangers watching the school? She'd heard other foster kids talk about the news and how kids went missing every day.

That men stole them and did mean things to them, and the kids never came back.

She jumped from the swing to go tell the teacher, but she stumbled again and her knee hit the ground. A big boy with a ball cap on laughed, and she frowned at him as she tried to get up.

Then the flash of the camera blinded her once more. When she finally could see again, the boy had run off and she was alone on the playground.

Alone except for the man in the car watching her... Was he one of the bad men the other fosters talked about?

Chapter Seven

Questions and doubts assailed Slade as they left Raleigh and headed back toward Sanctuary. Nash had seemed sincere in his concern for Nina.

But his condescending attitude had irritated the hell out of him.

Even though Nina had put on a brave face, hurt had laced her voice when she'd stood up to her father.

If anyone should have believed her, her own father should have. So why hadn't he?

Nina might be slightly obsessed over finding the truth about her daughter, but she didn't seem irrational or delusional. She also didn't appear to be taking drugs as her father had suggested.

And dammit, he understood her single-minded focus and the reason she'd asked questions. Obsession had driven him to keep looking for his sister until he'd located her.

And although he hadn't liked the outcome, at least he had closure. And his sister had received a decent burial.

Nina deserved to have closure, too.

Considering the fact that Nina was the only one who'd wanted the child, that left plenty of suspects. All who had means, motive and opportunity.

Her father. William Hood. Hood's mother.

Any one of them could have paid someone to kidnap the baby.

But they couldn't have predicted that the fire would break out the night Nina had delivered. Still, Nina's father and Hood might have come to the hospital when the baby was born, and jumped on the opportunity.

He frowned and maneuvered around traffic. And Hood's wife, Mitzi, topped his suspect list. Mitzi was upset about Nina's pregnancy. What if she'd been afraid William would change his mind after the baby was born and decide he wanted Nina and his daughter in his life?

Would she have been desperate enough to steal the baby?

Hood's mother was an even bigger question mark in his mind. She'd tried to bribe Nina to have an abortion. Had she kidnapped the baby so she wouldn't have to live with the stigma of an illegitimate child in the family? Or maybe she'd been worried that Nina might demand money. The baby would have had legal rights to the Hood fortune….

NINA STARED AT THE PASSING scenery, desperately trying to wrestle control over her ping-ponging emotions. She would not behave like the delusional psychotic her father and William had described.

"Nina?

She braced herself for Slade to announce he was dropping the case. "What?"

Slade slanted her a sideways look as he changed lanes. "Did your father come to the hospital when the baby was born?"

Fresh pain squeezed her heart. "The doctor called him. He was on his way when I went in to have the C-section."

"Did he see the baby?"

Emotions threatened to choke her as she remembered the harrowing birth. "No." She rubbed her temple in thought. "He didn't arrive until later, after the fire had broken out."

Slade twisted his mouth sideways. "What about Hood or any of his family members? Did they come to the hospital?"

She heaved a breath. "It may sound crazy after the way William treated me, but I did call him when I went into labor. I thought he had a right to know that his daughter was about to be born, that he might change his mind when he saw her."

A muscle ticked in his jaw. "But he didn't?"

"No. He ordered me to sign the papers and give her away, and not to ever bother him again."

"Cold son of a bitch," Slade muttered.

His comment eased some of the tension knotting her shoulders. "I remember thinking that myself. How could anyone be so unfeeling about their own child?"

A heartbeat of silence passed between them. "I don't know either," he said in a gruff voice. "But that apathy gives him motive."

"Does that mean that you're not dropping the investigation?"

The air vibrated with uncertainty and questions. "No, I'm not dropping it," he said. "I may not find the answers you want, but I am a man of my word, and I will get you answers."

SLADE REQUIRED VERY little sleep, but food was a different story. He pulled into the diner in town for a late lunch before heading to the hospital. He wanted to question the nurse on duty the night Nina had given birth.

It was way past the lunch hour, and the diner was nearly deserted, so they slid into a booth in the back. Slade ordered the deluxe burger and fries, and Nina a bowl of home-made soup. But she barely touched it.

"Have you had contact with William over the years?" he asked as he bit into his burger.

She sipped her tea. "Not really. I heard things through the gossip vine in town. About his graduation from law school, when he took over his Dad's practice. And I saw a write-up in the paper about his country-club wedding. Apparently it made the society page."

Climbing the social ladder seemed to be a high priority to the Hoods. But at what cost?

"You were in love with William?"

She shook her head and leaned her head on her hand, looking exhausted.

"No. I was young, Slade. Trying to fit in. Shy. And I was trying to impress my father."

"You went out with William to impress your father?"

A sarcastic laugh escaped her. "I realize that sounds ridiculous. But I was seventeen with no mother. More than anything I wanted my father to be proud. And the Hoods were the type of prestigious family he wanted me to end up with." She offered a self-deprecating smile. "So I was flattered when he asked me to prom. Then later…"

"Later what?"

"Later, I saw how selfish and conceited he was, and I didn't even like him, much less love him."

Slade ordered himself to resist the temptation to cover her hand with his, to soothe her distress.

But he lost the battle and did just as his heart commanded. Her hand felt small and cold and in need of a big one to cling to, and something twitched inside him urging him to be that someone. That everyone else in her life had let her down.

You might, too, a voice inside his head taunted.

Her fingers curled beneath the weight of his hand as if grasping on, and panic set in. He couldn't make promises to a vulnerable woman like her.

Not when he knew he'd walk away in the end.

He was too damn broken to be any good to anyone long-term.

She deserved someone better. A savior who'd stick around.

So he pulled his hand away and finished his burger in silence, determined to tie up the case so he didn't have to be tortured by her big, sad eyes, and by things he could never have or give her.

His cell phone buzzed as he was paying the bill, and he checked the number, saw it was GAI and connected the call. "Blackburn speaking."

"Slade, it's Amanda Peterson from GAI."

"Yeah?"

"Gage managed to get a copy of all the forensics reports from the hospital fire, including copies of the bodies found after the fire."

Slade's gut tightened. "And?"

"It was a mess," she said. "I can see why forensics and the cops had trouble sorting out the truth. Bodies were dismembered, literally blown apart. The chemicals ate away skin, bone and tissue, making identities impossible. The small town just didn't have the manpower at the time to handle such a large investigation, and the feds that came in wrote it off as a tragic accident and told families they had to accept the loss."

Slade saw Nina watching and adopted a poker face. "So what can you tell me?"

"They did take photographs of the bones and recorded the unidentified ones. Unfortunately hospital records were also destroyed that night, so any records of Peyton Nash, including her footprints and handprints, were lost in the fire."

"Damn."

A moment of silence, then Amanda continued. "But there were a couple of infant bones in the mix. I'm trying to see if they belong to Peyton now, but getting the results may take time."

"How about patient files of other births, infants in the hospital for other procedures, tests or treatments that night?"

"Gage already put Benjamin Camp on it."

Slade's admiration for McDermont rose. "Thanks. I'll fish around at the hospital. Keep me posted."

She agreed and he snapped his phone closed. Nina was watching with anticipation.

"What?"

"I told you I wouldn't mince words," Slade begun.

Her face paled slightly. "All right."

"The forensics expert at GAI is studying

copies of the forensics reports. I'm sorry to say, but there were infant bones in the mix."

Her breath hitched out. "Did they identify them?"

"No, they're working on that now. But I want to question Dr. Emery again. According to him, there weren't any babies other than Peyton lost that night."

Tears glittered in her eyes before she blinked them away. "Then he lied," she said with a strength to her voice that surprised him.

"Gage is going to request copies of hospital records from that night, but most were destroyed in the fire."

"Didn't they have some kind of back-up system?" Nina asked.

"Our computer guy is working on that angle." Slade reached for the bill. "Let's go talk to the nurse on duty that night and find out what she remembers."

THE IMPLICATIONS THAT there had been an infant's bones in the fire made Nina's stomach protest, and for a moment she'd thought she might lose the lunch she'd barely touched.

But she swallowed hard to stem the nausea. At least Slade hadn't given up. She'd asked for answers and she was grateful he was being honest with her, not treating her as if she were a crazy woman who might flip out if he didn't walk on eggshells around her.

The wind ruffled her hair as they entered the hospital and rode the elevator to the maternity floor. Nurses bustled up and down the halls, orderlies were picking up food trays, a woman in a robe strolled toward the nursery and voices echoed from the closest room nearby just as an older couple, probably grandparents, rushed down the hallway carrying flowers and a blue stuffed teddy bear.

Nina's experience had been so different, yet she had to smile at the thought of the happy couple and grandparents celebrating a new life.

"Excuse me," Slade said to a curly-haired nurse wearing pink scrubs at the nurses' station. "Is Carrie Poole here?"

The woman nodded. "She's in the NICU."

"Can you ask her if she can speak with us?" Slade asked.

The woman glanced at Nina with a frown. "Regarding what?"

Nina cleared her throat. "I just want to ask her a couple of questions. She took care of my baby when I was here a long time ago."

"You're Nina Nash, aren't you?" the woman asked.

Nina stiffened. "Yes."

"Dr. Emery said you hired a private investigator and were asking questions." A wariness tinged her eyes. "I wasn't here back then, but I've heard how horrible it was. I can't imagine…"

"I'm not here to cause trouble for the staff, or blame anyone for that night," Nina said. "In fact Carrie was so sweet to me, that I just want to talk to her, that's all. Please."

The woman's expression softened. "All right, sugar. I'll let her know."

She rose from the desk, exited on the opposite side and walked down the hallway.

Voices sounded, and she glanced to the left and saw a new mother cradling her baby as the nurse pushed her in a wheelchair toward the elevator. The father walked behind, carrying a bouquet of balloons and pink roses. As they reached the elevator, he leaned over and kissed his wife and baby girl. Tears stung Nina's eyes.

Slade's hand stroked her shoulder as if he understood how the scene affected her. A minute later, the nurse returned and pointed them to a waiting room. The bubbly redhaired nurse Nina remembered popped into the room a second later, and Nina made the introductions.

"I don't know if you remember me or not," Nina began.

"Of course I do." Carrie sat down and took her hands in hers. "I've thought about you a lot over the years. I'm sorry for all you've been through."

Her kindness touched Nina. "You were so sweet to me and my baby," Nina said. "I want to thank you for that."

Carrie smiled. "I can still see her little face, all scrunched up and fussing. She was a real fighter. I…thought she had a good chance." Carrie's voice cracked. "And then everything went wrong."

"Can you tell us exactly what you remember about that night?" Slade said.

She bit her lip as she looked at him, then nodded. "I wasn't in the nursery when the fire broke out. I was down the hall with another patient. I helped them to get out, then rushed back to help clear the babies. Two other nurses from the regular unit had infants in their arms, and rescue workers were rushing toward them to help. I ran to the NICU. There were only two babies in there that night, and Jane had the little boy. I went to get Peyton, but she wasn't in the bassinet."

"No one saw anyone take her?"

Carrie shook her head. "Dr. Emery had

ordered tests for the baby, and I assumed that someone had taken her to another wing to administer them."

"Carrie, I know it's been a long time," Slade said. "But do you remember anyone odd hanging around the nursery, someone who looked out of place?"

She fidgeted with the pocket of her scrubs jacket. "No, not that I can think of."

Slade hesitated. "How about other births that might have gone wrong that night or week? Maybe someone who had a miscarriage?"

Carrie drew her shoulders back. "That information is restricted for the patient's privacy."

"Please," Nina said. "If there's a chance another patient kidnapped my baby, you have to help me."

Her eyes flickered sideways nervously. "Well, there was one woman… She gave birth to a stillborn that afternoon. A baby boy."

Nina's chest constricted. "Do you remember her name?"

Carrie chewed her bottom lip. "I'm really not supposed to divulge that information. I could get fired." She fidgeted. "Besides, the poor woman suffered a terrible tragedy herself."

"I understand," Nina said. "What happened to the baby?"

"I don't know. He was probably taken for an autopsy."

"The woman's name?" Slade pressed.

"Gwen Waldorp," Carrie said. "I think she moved to Kings Mountain." Carrie glanced at her watch. "If that's all, I need to get back to work."

"One more question," Slade asked. "Do you know William Hood and his family?"

Carrie nodded. "I've seen their pictures in the newspaper."

"Were either William or his mother at the hospital the night Peyton was born?"

She backed away, fidgeting with her hair again. "I don't remember seeing them."

"How about William's wife? Her name is Mitzi."

"I told you I don't remember. It was madness here, everyone in a panic." She tapped her watch. "Now I really have to get back to work." Her ponytail swung behind her as she turned and rushed down the hall.

"What do you think?" Nina asked.

Slade frowned. "I think that nurse knows something she's not telling us." He gestured toward the elevator.

"That bone your forensics person found, it

could have belonged to the stillborn," Nina suggested.

He gave a clipped nod. "I'm going to check out this Waldorp woman and have a chat with William's mother."

Nina's thoughts raced as they took the elevator to the main floor, and Slade drove back to her house. Compassion for the woman who'd given birth to the stillborn baby squeezed her heart. Could she have been distraught enough to have kidnapped Peyton?

And William's mother...she'd been adamant that she should get rid of her baby. Could she have stolen her or hired someone else to and arranged for an adoption?

"Does Mrs. Hood live in Winston-Salem, too?"

Nina nodded.

"I'll question her tomorrow, but first I want to do some background work. I'm going to take that doll to the lab." Slade maneuvered around traffic through town, flipping on his windshield wipers as a light rain began to fall. "I'll also see if I can get an address for the Waldorp woman. I'll call you if I find anything."

Shadows flickered along the sidewalk, night setting in, the rain clouds adding to the gray fog over her house as he pulled into her drive.

Nina grasped on to hope as she climbed out and hurried up to her door. She went inside, flipped on the lights, then went upstairs to shower. A few minutes later, she dried off and pulled on a loose warm-up suit.

But the moment she went downstairs, the hair on the back of her neck stood on end, and panic hit her.

The CD of lullabies she'd bought for Peyton was playing.

And the baby blanket she'd crocheted and stored in the blanket chest in the attic was wrapped around another rag doll that had been stabbed just like the first.

Chapter Eight

Slade stopped by GAI and found Amanda Peterson still poring over forensics files. Benjamin Camp poked his head in when he saw Slade, and he brought them both up to speed on what he'd learned so far.

"You said a baby was stillborn that same day," Amanda said. "I'll find out if this bone could have belonged to that child instead of the Nash baby."

"Thanks," Slade said. "I'm sure it won't be easy."

Amanda grinned. "That's what I do," she said confidently. "Besides, if I can find out where the bone was located, that might help. And you said the stillborn was a baby boy?"

Slade nodded. "That will narrow things down. I'll make a phone call to the medical examiner and find out the names of any forensic specialists brought in to study the bones.

If they had a forensic anthropologist working with them, we should get some answers."

"I've been trying to dig up records on all the employees who worked at the hospital at the time," Benjamin said. "If the Hoods or Mr. Nash decided to arrange for an adoption, they might have hired someone to kidnap the baby."

"That's definitely a possibility." Slade heaved a breath. "Look for anyone with a shady past, a record, financial problems, anything that throws up a red flag." He remembered Carrie's nervous fidgeting. "Be sure to check out a nurse named Carrie Poole. She was on duty that night in the NICU."

"What's your next step?" Amanda asked.

"I'm going to investigate the Hoods, and William's wife, Mitzi. She dated William before Nina and was pissed when Nina turned up pregnant with his child."

"Sounds like motive to me," Benjamin muttered.

Slade sighed. "Yeah, although the nurse didn't remember seeing William or Mitzi at the hospital that night."

"You said yourself it was total chaos," Amanda commented. "With all the panic and rescue workers scrambling about, anyone could have slipped through and no one would have noticed."

"Something else is bugging me," Slade said. He removed the doll and showed it to them, then explained about the psychiatrist's report.

"Do you think she's unstable, that she put it there herself?" Benjamin asked.

Slade shifted on the balls of his feet. "No. At least she doesn't appear to be delusional." He decided to run with a theory. "But what if someone wanted everyone to think she was?"

Amanda drummed her fingers on the desk. "Then putting things in her apartment, like the lullaby CD and doll, that would remind her of her loss would do the trick."

Slade ran a hand over the back of his neck. It was devious, effective and cruel.

And he intended to find the son of a bitch who'd tormented her and make him suffer.

INSTINCTIVELY NINA REACHED inside her purse for her cell phone. She had to call Slade.

But after her father's comment and seeing the psychiatrist's report, she was afraid Slade wouldn't believe her.

The windowpane rattled upstairs, the floor creaking, and pure panic seized her.

What if the person who'd put the blanket on the rocker and started the CD was still inside?

The rain pounded harder, beating the roof, and suddenly the lights flickered off. Nina froze, listening, waiting.

But common sense kicked in, and she slowly slipped into the kitchen, pausing to listen for an intruder. The wind whistled through the eaves, the rain intensifying, and she eased open the door to the garage, scanning the darkness. A streak of lightning illuminated the interior, then suddenly a shadow moved across the window.

Terror streaked through her, and she ran to her car, jumped inside and locked the doors. Her hands shook as she dug her phone from her purse and tried to punch Slade's number. But she was trembling so badly she dropped the phone. She glanced at the window and saw a hand scraping across the fog-coated pane as if the man was reaching for her.

She screamed, bent to snap up the phone again then inhaled a deep breath to calm her nerves. She was locked in the car. The man was outside.

She was safe.

Finally she managed to punch in Slade's number. Again, she thought she saw the silhouette of the man race across the window, and her lungs squeezed, begging for air. The phone rang once, twice, then Slade's husky voice echoed over the line.

She clenched the phone close to her mouth. "Slade, someone was in my house," she whispered. "They're outside now."

"Where are you?"

"The garage." She scanned the window again. "In my car."

"I'll be right there."

The line went dead, and she clawed inside her purse and found her mace, bracing herself in case the man attacked.

SLADE SLAMMED ON HIS HORN, yelling at the cars to get out of the way. He wished to hell he had a siren to make the traffic move faster.

Nina might be in danger. He had to get to her, find out who was at her house.

Rainwater spewed from his tires, and he ground gears as he rounded a curve and sped onto the street leading to her house. As he neared the cul-de-sac, he searched the street and surrounding property.

His headlights flickered across the lawn, and he spotted a dog trotting by the mailbox.

Darkness shrouded Nina's house inside and out, sending alarm bells clanging in his head.

The rest of the neighborhood had lights.

Slowing, he pulled to the side and parked along the street, removed his weapon and crept toward her drive, glancing left and right in search of the intruder. The wind was blowing, tree branches swaying beneath the force, but the rain began to die down, turning to a drizzle.

His boots crunched wet leaves and twigs that had blown down in the storm as he inched forward. Moving slowly, instincts alert, he checked the front of the house. A streak of lightning zigzagged across the lawn, allowing him to see that no windows had been broken.

The intruder could have gotten in around back.

Slipping sideways, he padded around the outside of the house to the backyard. Woods backed up to the property, trees providing cover for someone who might have been inside and escaped.

He scanned the distance, but it was too dark to see into the trees. A twig snapping to the left made him jerk his head sideways, and a shadow moved. He raised his gun to fire, but a dog suddenly ran past, and he cursed. Dammit, he could have shot the animal....

Still tense, he made his way around the house, passing in front of the windows in the garage. Nina's car was parked inside, but the interior was dark and he couldn't see if she was still there.

Knowing he'd spook her if he knocked, he removed his phone and called her number.

She answered on the first ring. "Slade?"

"I'm outside. It's clear out here. Open the garage door and I'll search the house."

"I can't. It's electric," Nina said.

"There should be a button to switch it to manual."

"Yes," Nina said. "Let me find it."

A minute later, the garage door slid upward. Nina looked pale and shaken, and she was clenching a vial of mace in her trembling hands.

At least she'd had something to protect herself.

"You didn't find him?" she whispered.

"The only thing I saw was a dog."

"It wasn't a dog, Slade," Nina cried. "It was a man. I saw his hand on the window."

"How did you know he'd been inside?"

Pain flickered in her eyes. "He left me another present."

A curse rolled from his lips. "Stay here and let me make sure he's not still in the house."

She nodded, and he urged her inside the car again, then waited until he heard the lock click into place. Then he slipped inside the house to see what the bastard had left this time.

NINA RAKED HER fingernails up and down her arms, her nerves on edge as she waited for Slade to search the house. If the person who'd broken in and left that doll intended to scare her off, he was wrong.

She was stronger than she'd been eight years ago. And the fact that someone was tormenting her only made her believe that she was right about her daughter. That someone was scared she might discover the truth.

Because that person knew where her daughter was.

She glanced back and forth between the windows and door to the inside, her breath hitching when the door squeaked open. It was so dark, the only thing she could make out was the outline of a man's big body. Then the lights suddenly flickered on, and she recognized Slade.

He looked big and feral, his face chiseled into a hard mask. She flung open the car door, jumped out and hurried toward him.

He jammed his gun inside his jacket pocket and gripped her by the arms. "It's clear. The main breaker had been flipped. That's why the lights went out."

She nodded numbly, and allowed him to guide her into the kitchen, then into the den. Her gaze flew to the rocking chair and the doll wrapped in the baby blanket.

The lullaby CD was still playing, taunting her.

Slade clenched his jaw, then walked over and switched off the CD. "I'm going to send it to the lab although I doubt we'll get anything. Whoever did this probably wore gloves, but I'm still going to dust for prints."

Nina stared up at him, her heart racing. "Then you believe me? That I didn't put that creepy doll in the rocker or make up the intruder?"

His gaze met hers, emotions flickering in his brown eyes. Eyes that could dissect a person in seconds, eyes that could look cold and intimidating. Eyes that said he'd seen too much death and violence in his life.

She thought he wasn't going to answer, then

he cleared his throat. "Yes, Nina, I believe you."

His gruffly spoken words made her heart twinge, and suddenly tears filled her eyes. She'd been alone so long, had faced scorn and animosity and pity. She knew how to handle those.

She didn't know how to handle having someone believe in her again.

"God, Nina…" A groan ripped from his throat, then he pulled her in his arms and pressed her head to his chest.

Nina collapsed against him, savoring the feel of his strong arms embracing her. His heart thudded beneath her ear, his chest rose and fell with a labored breath and he gently stroked her hair. His touch felt so intimate that she clung to him, a flutter of arousal tickling her stomach.

Her breathing became raspy, her breasts tingled and she had the insane urge to press a kiss to his chest.

But that would be foolish. Just because he was being nice didn't mean he was attracted to her, or that he wanted her. He was simply being human, compassionate.

And she couldn't allow herself to lean on him

or become dependent. She'd learned long ago that men couldn't be counted on or trusted.

SLADE'S PULSE RACED. He shouldn't have pulled Nina up against him. It had been too damn long since he'd held a woman. Since he'd been with one.

Since he'd even wanted to.

But Nina had been trembling and afraid, and he'd seen the relief in her eyes that finally someone believed her story, and he couldn't resist.

Oh, hell… It was more than that.

She'd fought against all odds to find out what happened to her baby girl. How could he not admire her dedication and determination?

And now…one touch wasn't enough. Nina felt so small and sweet and precious in his arms that his body hardened, need ripping through him.

He traced his hand down her hair, then along her cheek. Her skin felt so soft that he wanted to put his lips where his fingers had just touched.

She tensed slightly as if to pull away, and he tilted her chin up with his thumb.

"I promise you I'll find out who's doing this," he said in a deep voice.

She nodded, her lower lip quivering. He traced his finger over her mouth, and her breath hitched, desire flaring in her eyes. "Slade…"

Her raspy sigh was his undoing.

He groaned, then lowered his head, angled his mouth and closed his lips over hers.

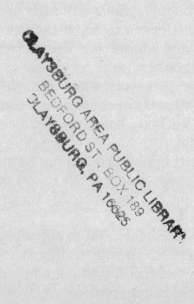

Chapter Nine

Slade traced his tongue along the seam of Nina's lips, urging her to open for him, and she complied. Her fingers tiptoed up his arm, and she threaded them in his hair, urging him closer, and another groan ripped from his gut.

Aching with the need to have her, he deepened the kiss, savoring the scent of her sweet body as she moved against him. Her lips tasted like berries and hunger, her kiss so erotic that flames of desire shot through him.

She moaned softly, her breasts brushing his chest in an erotic tease, and his hands slid downward to pull her hips deeper into the V between his thighs. He sucked her tongue into his mouth, greedy for more, and she trailed her hands down his arms to his back again, then slid one over his hip.

He wanted her to move that hand lower.

Then she pressed her lips over the scar on his cheek, and something moved inside him.

"What happened?" she whispered.

The images of his dying men flashed in his head. "Iraq."

"I'm sorry," she said, then traced her finger over the puckered skin.

Dammit. What the hell was he doing?

He tore himself away from her, well aware that they were both breathing heavily, on the verge of doing something each of them would regret.

"This is insane," he said, then forced himself to look away from the stormy heat in her eyes. If he didn't, he'd haul her back into his arms and this time he wouldn't stop. He'd carry her up the stairs, throw her down on the bed and make love to her until neither one of them could remember their names.

"Why is it insane?" Nina asked in such a sultry voice that he had to close his eyes to regain control.

"It just is."

"Why?" she asked again, this time hurt lacing her tone. "Because you think I'm unstable?"

God, he couldn't let her think that. "No. Because I'm working for you. This is a job, Nina. It can't be anything more."

Disappointment darkened her eyes, but he steeled himself and shut down.

He couldn't allow himself to care. Couldn't give her false promises or the impression that he'd stick around, that he was any kind of family man.

He didn't deserve a family, not after all the people he'd failed.

NINA SWALLOWED BACK her hurt. Slade was right.

They were working together, and she'd been frightened and had forgotten her senses for a moment.

It couldn't happen again.

Still, need and desire heated her blood, and she wished for once that she could feel something besides anguish and worry and the never-ending pit of emptiness inside her.

That she could feel loved.

But loving was dangerous. And the only person she had room for in her heart was Peyton. If—no *when*—she found her, her daughter would need all of her attention and time.

But what if she's happy with a loving family? Can you tear her away from a good home?

Her chest clenched, but she pushed away

the thoughts. She'd face that decision if it came down to it.

But the sound of Peyton's little voice taunted her. She wouldn't be able to hear that voice if Peyton wasn't calling out to her....

"Where did the baby blanket come from?" Slade asked, jarring her back to the present.

"I crocheted it for Peyton before she was born," Nina said. "But I packed it away in the storage closet in the guest room. That's where I stored all the baby things."

He narrowed his eyes. "So the intruder was in that room, and dug through your closet. I'll look for prints in there, too."

She nodded, then shivered at the thought of someone pawing through her precious baby items.

"Was there something special about that blanket?" Slade asked.

Nina pressed a hand to her mouth. "I was going to bring Peyton home in it."

A troubled look passed across his face. "Who knew about it?"

Nina frowned, trying to think back. "No one. At least I don't think anyone did. I made it when I lived alone here in Sanctuary."

"How about the CD?"

"One of the nurses who taught the prenatal classes gave each of the women a copy."

"What was the nurse's name?"

"Charlie," Nina said. "Why?"

"I'm just looking for a connection between the items and the person who broke in. For some significance."

Nina gave a small laugh. "Well, the psychiatrist said I played the CDs to soothe my grief, and the blanket to wrap my lost child in my love."

He slanted her an odd look. "I'm not sure I buy into that psychobabble."

"Thank you," she said softly. "That's the nicest thing anyone has said to me in years."

Her gaze locked with his, hope bubbling in her chest.

Hope and desire so strong that it scared her to death.

FOR A MOMENT, DESIRE flickered in Nina's eyes again, and Slade was tempted to pull her into his arms once more.

But his body still burned with need from her earlier touch, and his willpower couldn't tolerate the temptation. So he took a step back. "We should report this break-in to the sheriff."

"No." Panic tinged her voice. "I did that years ago, and look where it got me. Skepticism from everyone I talked to."

Slade hesitated. "All right. Let me retrieve the kit in my car and look for prints. I also want to figure out how the bastard got in here. And, Nina?"

"Yes?"

"Look around upstairs. Make sure nothing is missing."

She folded and unfolded her hands, her face strained. Looking at the baby items had to dredge up bad memories.

Which was exactly what her tormentor intended.

But she squared her shoulders and disappeared up the stairs. He strode out to his car and retrieved the crime kit GAI supplied. He'd take prints and if he found other evidence, he'd collect everything and send it all to the lab.

He grabbed a flashlight, and examined the front door, windows and back door and discovered that one of the locks on the window in the laundry room was broken. The intruder could easily have crawled in through the window.

Running the flashlight across the ground, he searched for footprints, but the rain had washed away any that might have been made earlier, and he didn't find any stray hairs or clothing fibers. Damn.

Next, he dusted the breaker box for prints, and found an index fingerprint. But it looked too small to be a man's. Probably Nina's. Still, he lifted it for comparison. He dusted the window in the laundry room from the outside, then inside, but again found nothing.

This guy was obviously smart enough to cover his tracks. After all, he'd done the same thing to Nina years ago.

It could be a woman, he reminded himself.

Or a hired crony.

Wiping perspiration from his forehead, he strode up the steps to the second floor and found Nina staring at a tiny pair of pink booties and a dress. God…

"Are you all right?"

"I'm fine," she said in a soft whisper. "I don't see anything missing."

A bittersweet look filled her eyes as she placed the dress back inside a plastic storage bin, and closed it. He dusted the closet door for prints, then the bin. Only one set, which he assumed belonged to Nina.

"Did you find anything outside?" she asked.

"The lock on the window in your laundry room is broken. The intruder must have climbed through it."

Nina nodded. "I didn't realize. I'll go fix it now."

He caught her arm as she stood and stopped her before she could go down the steps. "No, you look exhausted. Go lie down. I'll fix the window and stay on the couch tonight."

Nina rubbed her forehead. "You don't have to do that, Slade."

"Yes, I do," he said. "This guy might come back."

A shudder coursed through her, and he hated himself for scaring her.

"Thank you," she said softly.

"Stop thanking me," he muttered. "I'm just doing my job."

She shifted, her mouth tightening. "Right." Then she rushed into her own room and shut the door. For a moment, he stood rooted to the spot. The temptation to go inside with her taunted him.

What would she do if he knocked and asked to join her? Would she let him hold her? Kiss her? Make love to her?

Damn. This case was starting to feel like more than just a job. He didn't want to see her hurt anymore. And seeing that tiny little dress made him want to bring her child home to her.

But he couldn't get physically involved

with her any more than he could emotionally. That would distract him from the case. And knowing that an intruder had broken in and might return meant he had to stay sharp and focused.

He took the steps two at a time, found a tool kit in the garage and repaired the broken lock. Then he retrieved his computer from his SUV, and booted it up at her kitchen table.

He'd set up watch for the night. And if the intruder came back, he'd catch the son of a bitch and make him sorry for tormenting Nina.

NINA WRESTLED WITH SLEEP, the images of the doll wrapped in Peyton's baby blanket haunting her.

She pulled the covers to her chin, hating the silence. But knowing Slade was downstairs made her feel safer.

Don't get used to it, she reminded herself. *When you find your daughter, he'll leave and you'll be alone again.*

No, she wouldn't. She'd have her little girl, and that would be enough.

With that thought on her mind, she finally fell asleep and dreamed that she had Peyton back, and that she'd taken her to the zoo. Peyton's blond curls bounced around her face as she giggled at the chimpanzees squawking and jumping up and down and chomping on bananas.

The lions' roar frightened her, and she scrunched close to Nina, and Nina smoothed her hair down and hugged her. Then a crowd gathered by the giraffes and they walked over to join them.

Suddenly Slade appeared, the sunlight gleaming off his strong jaw and rugged body. He smiled at her, then swung Peyton up onto his shoulders so she could see over the crowd.

Peyton clapped her hands and shrieked with glee. "I'm almost as tall as the giraffes," Peyton said. "Lift me higher, Daddy, and I can eat from the treetops."

Slade chuckled and pulled Nina next to him, and a warmth enveloped her. She loved her husband and her daughter and finally had the family she'd always wanted.

Then suddenly a dark cloud fell over the crowd, and she looked up and Peyton and Slade were gone. She cried out their names, frantically searching, but she'd lost them….

No, she heard Peyton singing again.

She jerked awake, the sound of her daughter's voice echoing through the room and sending a blinding pain through her chest.

Her breathing was ragged, and she crawled from the bed, walked to the window and looked up at the moon. "I'm going to find you, baby," Nina whispered. "I promise. I'll find you and bring you home and one day we'll take that trip to the zoo."

Only Slade wouldn't be around. Peyton wouldn't have a daddy.

But she would make up for it by loving her enough for two parents.

SLADE LOOKED UP THE HOOD family and found numerous articles on William's father's law practice, his tragic death from cancer, and articles featuring William's graduation from law school, the honors he'd received and the cases he'd handled.

Apparently, William was a cutthroat lawyer who handled high-finance and tax cases and had made a fortune. Photographs of his society wedding to Mitzi Raynor, the daughter of a prominent judge, highlighted the young couple's budding social life.

Another photo depicted the celebration of Mrs. Hood's fiftieth birthday celebration a few months before. Slade studied the brassy-haired woman in her perfect outfit with her perfect smile, perfect face and perfect family.

Beneath that perfect veneer, beat the heart of an ugly barracuda.

The woman had tried to bribe Nina to abort her own grandchild, then urged her to give the baby up for adoption. Was she cunning enough to plan a kidnapping to spare the family the stigma of an illegitimate child?

His frown deepened as he scrolled farther down and zeroed in on a photo—one that included William, his sister, Diane, and her husband, Dennis, and their daughter.

His shoulders cramped with tension as he studied the little girl huddled between Diane and her husband. A little girl who looked about eight years old. A blonde…

The same age as Peyton…

REBECCA WAS RUNNING, running, running, as fast as she could. She had to get away from the bad men.

He'd watched her at school and taken pictures. And now he'd followed her to the house.

But her legs were weak, and she stumbled. He snagged her arm, and she screamed, beating her fists against him. "Let me go, let me go."

He shook her. "Stop it!"

"No, let me go!"

"Rebecca, wake up."

"No, they're going to get me…"

He shook her harder, so hard her teeth rattled. "Wake up. You just scratched me, you little twerp."

Rebecca jerked her eyes open and stared at the darkness. The voice…it belonged to her foster father. His breath smelled nasty as he glared at her.

"You were dreaming, kid, screaming and carrying on." He released her and she fell back against the bed as he stood. "I don't want to hear any more from you, you hear me?"

"But the man from school, he was watching and he came after me…"

"I said hush." He raised one fist as if he was going to hit her. "Do you hear me?"

Terrified, Rebecca bit her tongue to keep from screaming, then slowly nodded.

The bed creaked as he lifted his bulk. Then the floor squeaked as he shuffled back to the door. He stopped at the doorway and turned back to her. "I mean it, kid. I'd better not hear another sound out of you."

Rebecca clenched the covers to her neck and nodded again, holding her breath until he shut the door.

She blinked hard, and pressed her hands to

her eyes to keep from crying. She wouldn't cry. She was a big girl now.

A scraping sound echoed in the room, and she gripped the covers and slowly twisted her head sideways to look at the window.

Scrape. Scrape. Scrape. Something was out there. Something that sounded like claws.

Was it a wild animal? Or had the mean man in her nightmares really found her?

Chapter Ten

Nina sat up and stared into the darkness. Peyton's singing had stopped.

In fact she was crying. Peyton was scared of something—or someone.

A helpless ache engulfed her, fueling her anger, and she turned her face up to the heavens. "Where is she? God, please, I'm not crazy, am I? My daughter needs me."

Downstairs, she heard footsteps, remembered Slade and breathed in relief.

More determined than ever, she quickly showered, then hurried down the steps. The scent of coffee wafted toward her, and she found Slade gripping a mug in his hand when she entered the kitchen.

His gaze raked over her and made her body tingle. "Did you sleep?"

"A little," she admitted. "But then the nightmares came."

He nodded, his expression hooded, then

stepped aside while she poured herself a cup of coffee.

Last night she'd lost her head and let her emotions overwhelm her. Today, she'd keep their conversation focused on the investigation.

And she'd keep her hands to herself. No more reaching for him or letting him hold her. No more kisses.

No use in fantasizing about something that she could never have.

"I located an address for Gwen Waldorp," Slade said. "I'm going to see her this morning."

Nina sipped her coffee, her stomach churning. Questioning Gwen would resurrect painful memories for her. But if she hadn't kidnapped Peyton, she might have seen something, heard something… "All right."

"Then we'll go see William's mother and sister."

Nina narrowed her eyes. "His sister?"

He gestured toward his computer, and she glanced at the photos he'd accessed. "She has a daughter the same age as Peyton."

Nina studied the photo of the little blonde, her mind racing. "No wonder Mrs. Hood was so callous about William having an illegitimate child. She was already going to be a grandmother."

Slade shrugged. "Maybe."

His tone made her pause, and she glanced at the child again. Blond hair, freckles…the same age as Peyton.

Her breath stammered in her chest. What was Slade thinking? Did he suspect that little girl might be Peyton?

"Did you know Diane?" Slade asked.

She shook her head. "No, she was four years older than me and already married."

"Were you aware she was expecting a baby the same time you were?"

Nina swallowed. "No. William never mentioned it…" Her voice warbled. "Slade, do you think…?"

"I don't know," he said, obviously reading her mind. "But it's worth looking into."

Nina agreed, placed her coffee cup in the sink and went to retrieve her purse. She locked the house securely, and she and Slade drove to the mountains. Antique stores, craft shops, a diner, a candy shop and majestic scenery gave the town a quaint feel.

Gwen Waldorp lived in a cottage-style house with white latticework, a glider on the front porch and a bird feeder in the yard. Evidence that kids lived there was everywhere, from the tricycle to the football to the pink scooter.

A pink scooter—Gwen had a little girl, too....

Nerves fluttered in Nina's stomach as she walked up the flower-lined path to the front door. Slade punched the bell, and a moment later, the patter of little feet sounded from inside.

Then the door opened, and her heart squeezed at the sight of the child.

A towheaded little boy about three with bright green eyes.

"Who're you?" He scrunched his nose, revealing a missing front tooth.

"We'd like to see your mommy," Slade asked. "Is she here?"

"Mommy!" the boy shouted. "A giant man and a wady are here!"

"Bobby, I told you not to open the door to strangers," the woman called as she rushed into the room. A dark-haired little girl tagged close behind her, her face streaked with something that looked like chocolate pudding.

"Hi," Nina said, smiling at the little girl. "My name is Nina. What's yours, honey?"

The little girl bobbed from foot to foot, then whispered, "Judy."

"How old are you, Judy?" Nina asked.

Judy smiled. "Eight. I just had a birthday and got a new bike."

Gwen pushed the child behind her like a mother protecting her cub. "Who are you and what do you want?"

Nina scrutinized the child's features, comparing her heart-shaped face to Gwen's, and trying to remember what her own childhood photographs had looked like. Judy's hair was slightly darker than her mother's sandy color, but she didn't have Nina's blond hair either, and her eyes were hazel, not blue.

Still… Could Judy possibly be her daughter?

"Mrs. Waldorp," Slade began. "This is Nina Nash, and my name is Slade Blackburn with Guardian Angel Investigations."

A frown creased Gwen's forehead. "How can I help you?"

Nina wet her dry lips with her tongue. "I'd like to talk to you about the hospital fire in Sanctuary eight years ago. You probably read that the sheriff arrested the men responsible for the explosion."

Gwen's face blanched. "Yes, but what does that have to do with me? I didn't know any of them."

"We're not accusing you of having anything to do with the fire," Slade said.

"Then what's going on?" Gwen asked. "Why dredge up that night? It was a bad time for me."

Nina pressed her hand over the woman's. "I understand, but this is important. Please."

Grief darkened Gwen's eyes, and she seemed to be debating on whether to continue. But then she leaned down and stroked her daughter's hair. "Judy, why don't you take Bobby into the den and watch cartoons. Mommy will be there in a minute."

"'Kay, Mommy." The little girl had been watching with avid curiosity, but she grabbed her brother's hand and they raced away.

"Come in," Gwen said, then gestured toward the kitchen. The room adjoined the den so she could keep an eye on the kids. She offered them coffee, and Slade accepted although Nina's stomach was somersaulting so she declined.

"We understand that you lost a child the same night as the fire," Nina said. "Your baby was stillborn."

Gwen massaged her temple as if the memory were still raw. "Yes. How did you know?"

"Because I was there. I lost a child that night, as well." Nina explained about her own labor and delivery, and her frantic search to find her daughter.

"I'm sorry." Gwen's voice trembled. "But what does this have to do with me?"

"Forensics never found my baby's body," Nina said. "I think she might still be alive."

Suddenly the woman's eyes flashed with surprise. "What?"

"I know it's a long shot," Nina continued. "But in the chaos, I think someone might have taken her."

Gwen's expression shifted from curiosity to anger at the sudden realization of their implications. "Oh, my God. You think I stole your baby?" she asked in an incredulous tone. She glanced at her daughter. "That's why you asked Judy how old she was."

Slade planted his hands on the table. "We're exploring every angle, no matter how remote," Slade said.

Gwen stood with a hiss. "I think you'd better leave."

"Mrs. Waldorp," Slade said calmly. "We've reviewed the forensics reports. There is an infant's bone in the report, but no ID. What happened to your child? Was your baby's body recovered?"

Anguish flashed on Gwen's face. "No, I… didn't even get to bury him…" She inhaled a deep breath, then straightened as if logging the memory away.

"Judy is eight," Slade pointed out. "You couldn't have given birth to her."

"She's adopted, isn't she?" Nina asked.

Gwen's lips compressed. "That's none of your business."

"Please," Nina pleaded.

Gwen sank back into the chair and fiddled with a napkin on the table. "Yes, she's adopted. But we went through the lawyer in town, and it was perfectly legal."

"Do you know who Judy's birth parents are?" Slade asked.

She lowered her voice. "Yes. The baby's mother died in the fire that night. When we heard about the baby, and learned the woman had no family, we jumped in to take Judy. She needed us and we needed her."

"She seems small for her age," Slade said. "Did she have any health problems when she was born?"

Gwen glanced at her daughter, concern on her face. "She has asthma. Why?"

"My baby was premature," Nina said. "She was in the NICU."

"Judy is not your child, Miss Nash." Gwen folded her arms, her expression shutting down. "Now, I've answered your questions because

I feel sorry for you. But I think it's time for you to leave."

"I'm sorry," Nina said. "But I'm desperate to find out what happened to my baby. Do you think it's possible that the lawyer lied to you when he claimed Judy's mother died in the fire?"

Gwen ripped the napkin in two. "Why would he do that?"

Nina explained about the Hoods' reactions to her pregnancy.

Gwen's eyes widened. "You're suggesting that one of them kidnapped your baby, then gave her to me?"

"It's one theory," Slade said matter-of-factly.

Gwen stood. "Well, that's just not possible. Judy can't be your child. Her mother is dead."

Nina glanced back at the little girl. She was precious, but she didn't feel the connection she'd expected to feel when she saw her child again for the first time. Did that mean Judy wasn't hers? That Gwen was telling the truth?

"Then maybe you saw something that night that can help me," Nina continued. "Maybe you saw someone strange hanging around the nursery…"

Gwen folded her arms, then cast her a belligerent look. "I'm afraid I can't help you. I was so distraught over my loss that the nurses gave me a sedative. I barely remember the fire, only that someone carried me outside."

She ran a shaky hand through her hair. "Now, I really do want you to leave. I have my family to take care of."

NINA'S SILENCE DURING the drive toward Winston-Salem worried Slade. He understood that the interview with the Waldorp woman was uncomfortable, but asking questions always caused some kind of emotional reaction. It was part of the job.

Besides, he didn't give a damn what anyone thought of him. He had to ask questions, probe, pry, piss off people, sometimes lie or treat them harshly to get answers.

But Nina had a compassionate nature, and her empathy for the other woman would have clouded her judgment.

"Do you believe her story?" Slade asked.

Nina shrugged. "It sounds plausible."

"Yeah," Slade said. "But she might not know the truth herself. If someone paid the doctor enough, he could have fabricated that story and given her your baby and merely told her the baby's mother died to avoid questions and to push the adoption through without questions."

Nina leaned her head into her hands. "It's hard for me to wrap my mind around the fact that someone could be that devious." Her expression grew more strained. "And the little girl did look happy. Gwen obviously loves her like she was her own."

Slade gritted his teeth. Yes, the woman did. But was the child Nina's? He needed DNA for verification, and Gwen Waldorp wouldn't give that up easily.

Nina looked so distraught he wanted to take her in his arms and hold her again, assure her everything was all right. But if that child was Nina's, then she would be torn over what to do.

And ripping the child away from the only mother she'd ever known, and her father and baby brother, would be hell for everyone.

Dammit.

He glanced at Nina again. How was she going to handle a confrontation with Mrs. Hood, the woman who'd tried to pay her to get rid of her child?

Slade's cell phone buzzed, and he connected the call. "Blackburn."

"It's Amanda. I talked to the forensic anthropologist and she reviewed her files. That infant bone belonged to a baby boy, not Peyton Nash."

Probably Gwen's stillborn child. Slade thanked her again and disconnected the call, then relayed the forensics findings.

Nina chewed her bottom lip. "Then it wasn't Peyton. That means she's alive."

Slade slanted her a warning look. "It means there's no proof that she was caught in the fire, Nina." And he needed more before a judge would grant a request for Judy Waldorp's DNA.

"She's alive," Nina said with such certainty that he almost believed that she really knew, that she might have some kind of connection to her daughter.

But he had long ago lost faith in anything, much less something intangible like love or a connection between two people. Even a mother and daughter.

He found the country-club community where William's mother lived, stopped at the security gate, showed his ID, then drove past the manicured golf course to the Hood estate, a massive English Tudor house that looked more like a hotel than a home.

A crew of workers were busy tending the lawn and flower beds and looked up when he parked, but didn't comment as he and Nina walked up the walkway.

He rang the doorbell, tapping his foot as he waited. Finally a woman in a uniform answered. "Is Mrs. Hood in?" Slade asked.

"No, sir, I'm sorry. May I tell her who was inquiring?"

"Where is she?" Slade asked.

The woman frowned. "I don't give out her whereabouts to just anyone."

"Please," Nina said, then introduced the two of them. "It's important I talk to her."

The woman hesitated but her look softened. "She's at the country club having lunch."

Nina thanked her, and the two of them returned to the SUV. Slade circled back the way they'd come and pulled into the parking lot of the country club.

"Mrs. Hood won't be pleased to see us," Nina said.

Slade grunted. "I don't give a damn. From what I've heard about this lady, she deserves to be knocked down a peg or two."

A small smile curved Nina's mouth, making him see for the first time how beautiful she would be if she were happy. He wanted to see her smile again.

Marble floors gleamed as they walked in, the scent of fresh flowers filling the entry.

Beveled mirrors, expensive paintings and vases decorated the walls, and heavy, red velvet curtains covered the windows.

To the right, he spotted a plush dining room, and he and Nina walked to the doorway. The room was packed with women's groups, couples and businessmen, most dressed to the nines. An outdoor patio held other tables where the tennis and golf crowd seemed to have gathered.

"She's in the far-right corner," Nina said, pointing to a small table of four women.

Slade gestured for her to lead the way, and she crossed the room, silently willing herself to remain strong and not let the woman rattle her. When Mrs. Hood noticed them, she jumped up, shock and anger drawing her face into a scowl. She tossed down her napkin and strode briskly from her party, weaving between white-linen-clothed tables until she reached them.

She stopped and glared at Nina, her diamonds twinkling beneath the crystal chandelier. "What are *you* doing here?"

Nina squared her shoulders. "Trying to find my daughter."

Mrs. Hood rolled her eyes. "My God, it's true," she huffed. "William called and warned me you'd hired another P.I."

"Yes, I have," Nina said flatly. "And I'm not going to give up until I learn the truth."

The woman's eyes spewed rage as she tossed her head back. "Well, I have *nothing* to say to you."

Slade cleared his throat. "We can talk here, lady, in front of your friends or step into the hall for privacy. Your choice. But we will talk."

Mrs. Hood snarled then strutted toward the lobby, her heels clicking on the polished marble floors. Obviously determined to avoid a scene, she led them to a small alcove, then folded her arms, gold bracelets clinking on her wrists. "You have five minutes before I call security and have you removed from the premises."

Nina pressed her lips into a tight line, and Slade gritted his teeth. He'd never hit a woman before, but he felt like slugging this one. "Where were you last night, Mrs. Hood?"

An appalled gasp escaped her. "At the club. Why?"

"Because since I started investigating this case, someone has started taunting Nina."

"Don't let her fool you, Mr. Blackburn. She's delusional and can't accept the fact that her child died."

Slade straightened to his full height,

towering over her and pinning her with an intimidating stare. "I think she has good reason to suspect that her daughter might have survived."

"What are you talking about? The police turned up nothing—"

"Exactly," Slade said. "They never found a body."

"Good heavens," Mrs. Hood said, sounding exasperated. "Just look at the horrible pictures from that fire. The baby certainly didn't walk out alive on her own."

Slade shoved his face into hers. "No, she didn't. I think you or someone you hired carried her out."

Chapter Eleven

At one time the vehemence in William's mother's voice would have bothered Nina, but she no longer cared about the woman's opinion.

And if she had been responsible for Peyton's disappearance, she would never forgive her.

Mrs. Hood's eyes widened. "How dare you imply such a thing?"

"You tried to bribe Nina to have an abortion," Slade continued. "And when she refused, you tried to convince her to give the baby up for adoption."

"She was just a child herself, a little tramp, not equipped to take care of a baby," Mrs. Hood said icily.

"Oh, come on," Slade said in a tone that matched the woman's. "You weren't concerned about the baby, or you would have offered to help raise her. You just didn't want a reminder that your son had an illegitimate child."

She batted her false eyelashes. "That's ridiculous."

Slade arched a brow. "Is it? Or does the truth sound as ugly as it is, because it certainly sounds like you had motive for kidnapping."

"I did not kidnap that child," Mrs. Hood said vehemently.

"Then tell me where you were the night the baby disappeared."

"I don't know who you think you are, Mister, but I don't have to tell you anything."

Slade shifted and crossed his arms. "Were you at the hospital the night Nina gave birth?"

Mrs. Hood lifted her chin haughtily. "Either leave now, or I'm calling security."

Nina touched her arm. "Were you at the hospital, Eileen?"

"No." Mrs. Hood jerked her arm away from Nina's hand. "For heaven's sakes, stop harassing me."

"Then you hired someone," Slade suggested. "Did you arrange for an adoption or did your own daughter take the baby and raise her?"

Mrs. Hood gasped and raised her hand as if

she might slap Slade. "You leave my daughter and grandchild out of this. Now get out!"

Her raised voice and demeanor caught a security guard's attention and he strode toward them.

Slade made a sarcastic sound low in his throat. "Lady, you don't scare me."

"You should be scared, Mr. Blackburn. I have a lot of money and power in this town, and I can sue you for harassment."

Slade held up a hand to the approaching security guard, indicating that force wasn't necessary. "I don't give a damn who you are or how much money you have, Mrs. Hood. If you did something to Nina's child, I'll find out, and you will rot in prison." He glanced across the ballroom with disdain. "And you won't be dining on caviar or wearing diamonds there."

"THANK YOU FOR STANDING up for me in there," Nina said as they walked out to his SUV.

Slade grimaced as he climbed inside and started the engine. "That woman is a snotty bitch."

Nina laughed, a musical sound that made Slade pause and look at her. With the afternoon sunlight dancing through the silky strands of her blond hair and that smile, she looked radiant.

His gut pinched, his body hardening instantly. He wanted to touch her hair again, kiss those perfect, ripe lips and run his hands over her body.

He wanted to solve all her problems.

That thought sent a surge of fear through him. He was getting too close to her, starting to care.

Caring was dangerous.

Gritting his teeth, his resolve set in. *Stay focused. Keep your mind on the case.*

Find the little girl and get away from Nina.

He just hoped to hell he found her alive….

His stomach growled, and he drove to downtown Winston-Salem, and found a café for lunch. Nina ordered a salad and he wolfed down a burger.

"I still can't believe Mrs. Hood would kidnap my baby and keep her from me all these years."

"I can't believe you'd even doubt it. The woman is obsessed with money and her image."

"That's true." Nina nodded and sipped her

water. "And she definitely wanted me out of her life."

"If you'd kept the baby, she was probably afraid you'd try to milk the family for money."

Nina gasped. "I would never have done that, Slade."

"I didn't mean to imply you would. But your child would have been a rightful heir to the Hood fortune, and William would have owed you child support for years." He lifted a brow. "This way, they were free and clear."

"She didn't care how much she hurt me," Nina said quietly. "And those dolls...do you think she could have put them in my house?"

"I doubt she'd dirty her own fingers," Slade said. "But with her money, she could have hired someone to make you look crazy so no one would believe you."

"And it worked," Nina said. "Even my father thought I'd lost my mind, that I did those things myself."

Slade shrugged, then settled the bill, and they went back to the car and headed toward William's sister's house.

"If Mrs. Hood is guilty, I wonder if William knew what she did," Nina said.

Slade gritted his teeth. "If he did, they'll all pay for it."

Nina lapsed into silence until they reached their destination, a modern brick two-story in an upper-class neighborhood. The Lucases were obviously doing well for themselves. From the article he'd read online, he'd learned that Mr. Lucas was a physician at the local hospital.

Slade punched the doorbell, and the sound of footsteps echoed from inside. A thin blonde wearing shorts and a tank top answered the door.

"Mrs. Lucas?" Slade said.

The woman's expression was wary. "Yes. My mother called. I've been expecting you, Nina." She gestured for them to come in. "Let's go out back. Tiff is in the pool, and I need to watch her."

"Of course," Nina and Slade said at the same time.

They followed her through an immaculate kitchen and sunroom to a brick patio and pool. The little girl was playing with a dinosaur raft in the water. Longing swelled in Nina's eyes.

"Mother claims that you accused her of kidnapping your baby eight years ago," Diane said. "Is that true?"

"We just wanted to ask her some questions," Slade began, then explained their reasoning behind believing Peyton might still be alive.

"I see." Diane gave Nina a sympathetic look. "I can't imagine what you've been through," she said in a low voice then turned to look at her daughter who was laughing as she struggled to climb on the raft. "I don't know what I would have done if I were in your shoes, but I'd probably be asking the same questions."

Slade was surprised at her calm sensitivity. This woman seemed nothing like her mother.

"Diane," Nina said, "I hate to ask you this, but your mother hated me back then, and she didn't want me to have the baby. She offered me a bribe to have an abortion."

Diane sighed and glanced down at her hands, then looked back up. "I know. William told me. And I have to admit that I wasn't surprised. Mother has always been obsessed about her reputation and climbing the social ladder."

"In light of how she felt," Slade said, "do you think she might have arranged for someone to take the baby?"

The little girl squealed and Diane glanced at her to make sure she was okay. But Tiff had managed to straddle the dinosaur and was laughing with glee, splashing and paddling with all her might.

"I don't know," Diane said. "I'd hate to think my mother would do something that devious. I...just can't imagine."

A car sounded in the drive out front, and footsteps pounded through the house. A moment later, a dark-haired man in a suit appeared through the French doors, looking furious.

"Diane, what in the hell are you doing letting these people in our house?"

Diane stood. "Calm down, Dennis. There's no reason I shouldn't talk to them."

Dennis stormed over to the patio table where they were sitting. "This is outrageous. Your mother called me, hysterical. She said they accused her of kidnapping a child and then giving the baby to us to raise."

"I'm sorry," Nina said. "I'm just trying to piece together what happened to my little girl."

"Look, Miss Nash," Dennis said, lowering his tone. "Your baby died. It was sad, tragic even, but you have no right to accuse us of kidnapping."

"Can you prove that little girl is your birth child?" Slade asked.

Fury radiated from Lucas's pores. "Of course I can. She was born in the same hospital where I work. I was a resident then and helped deliver her myself." He jammed his hands on his hips. "And before you ask, yes, I have the birth certificate to prove it."

"Papers can be doctored," Slade said with an eyebrow raised. "You're a doctor. You certainly have the power and connections to do it."

"This is unbelievable," Dennis shouted.

The little girl stopped splashing and stared at them, and Diane grabbed her husband's arms. "Calm down, Dennis. You're scaring Tiff."

Dennis cut his eyes toward the little girl, then inhaled a calming breath and spoke through clenched teeth. "I'll calm down when these people get off my property."

"If the little girl is yours," Slade said in a low voice, "then you can easily prove it by giving us a DNA sample."

"I'll do no such thing," Dennis snarled. "Now leave before I call the police and file harassment charges."

Slade returned his stare with a cool mask. "We'll leave for now. But your decision not to cooperate only makes you look guilty."

"I'm protecting my family and well within

my rights," Dennis said. "Now get out before I throw you out myself."

NINA BACKED AWAY AT the rage in Dennis Lucas's eyes.

Diane placed her hand on her husband's shoulder. "I'll walk them to the door, Dennis. Stay here, have a beer and watch Tiff."

He stared at them for another long moment. "You don't need a P.I., you need a shrink, Miss Nash. Go see one, and don't bother us again."

Slade started to speak, but Nina took his arm. "Let's go, Slade."

The men continued the silent stare-off for another second, then Slade conceded with a nod. "If I find out you're lying about any of this," he said, "I'll be back."

Nina tugged him through the sunroom door, then Diane guided them back into the kitchen. But she stopped and picked up a hairbrush, then gave Nina a sympathetic look.

"This brush belongs to Tiff. Take your DNA and you'll see that Tiff is not Nina's child."

Nina gasped in surprise. "Why are you helping us?"

Diane squeezed Nina's arm. "Because I'm a mother, and if it will put your mind to rest, then I understand. I never approved of the way my mother and brother treated you."

Tears burned the back of Nina's eyes. "I… don't know what to say." She glanced at Slade, thinking they didn't need to take the sample.

But Slade plucked a couple of hair strands from the brush and dropped them into a small envelope he had inside his jacket before she could respond, then Diane escorted them to the front door.

"I hope you find what you're looking for," Diane said.

Nina thanked her again, moved by her understanding and compassion.

She and Slade walked back to his SUV in silence, but as soon as she settled in the passenger seat, she spoke. "I don't think Diane had anything to do with Peyton's disappearance."

"You're too trusting, Nina."

She gave a self-deprecating laugh. "Not really. But she seemed genuine, and she did offer up the DNA."

Slade started the engine, and pulled out into the subdivision and headed back toward Sanctuary. "Still, her husband's reaction made me wonder."

"Wonder what?"

"Even if Tiff is theirs, he might know something. Mrs. Hood could have asked for his help in doctoring paperwork or arranging for an adoption."

Nina leaned her head against the headrest. "And if Peyton was adopted, the records are probably sealed, so I may never know where she is."

Slade covered her hand with his. "If Lucas was complicit, I'll force him to talk. Finding out which adoption agency, especially if it's a private agency, and the name of the lawyer who handled the adoption, would be a lead."

Nina's emotions bounced between hope and despair. "That is, if they used a lawyer. For all we know, Mrs. Hood paid someone to steal Peyton and take her away. She might not even be in the country." Nina's throat clogged with fear. She'd tried not to let her imagination travel that route, but she had to face reality.

Slade's closed look confirmed she could be right. This investigation might only lead them to a certain point, and then the trail could turn cold.

She closed her eyes, willing her courage to return. But suddenly Slade cursed, and yanked the SUV sideways.

She jerked her eyes open, and saw a car racing up too close behind them.

"What's wrong?" Nina asked.

"That car nearly hit us a minute ago."

They were approaching a bridge over a bypass, and suddenly the car roared closer again, and this time sped up and passed them.

"Dammit," Slade muttered as he hit the brakes to avoid slamming into it. But instead of slowing, his car accelerated.

He pumped the brakes, tightening his fingers around the steering wheel in a white-knuckled grip. But the SUV flipped up on two wheels, tires squealing.

"Slade—"

"Hold on, the brakes aren't working!"

An oncoming car blared its horn when he crossed the line, and Slade jerked the car to the right, skimming the guardrail.

Sparks flew, the sound of metal scrunching rent the air, then the SUV slammed into the side and spun out of control.

Nina screamed and Slade cursed as they careened over the side of the bridge, hit the pavement below and began to roll.

Chapter Twelve

Slade's chest pounded as the car spun upside down and skidded toward another vehicle. Metal screeched. Glass shattered. The air bags exploded, popping him in the face and chest, and the front of the car was crunched so tight, he couldn't move his legs.

Dammit. He needed to get them out.

He glanced sideways to see if Nina was all right, but she wasn't moving.

"Nina, honey, are you okay?" He struggled to find her hand and squeezed her fingers. "Nina, talk to me. Are you all right?"

Fear seized him when she didn't respond.

He dug in his pocket, found his Swiss army knife, flipped it open and ripped at his air bag, then hers until he could see her face. She looked so pale that sweat beaded on his skin. A scrape marred one cheek, and blood dotted her forehead. "Nina, baby, you have to talk to me."

But she still didn't respond.

Frantically he felt for his phone, but before he could punch 9-1-1, a siren wailed, and he realized someone else had called in the accident.

Or had it been an accident? His brakes had completely failed….

Nina moaned, and he angled his upper body sideways. His legs were trapped, his right knee throbbing, but at least he could feel them, so that was a good sign. He gently stroked her cheek.

"Nina, wake up, honey. We've been in an accident."

Slowly she opened her eyes, but they looked glazed and disoriented.

"We crashed," Slade said. "But I hear sirens, so an ambulance will be here soon. Where are you hurt?"

She frowned, lifted a scraped hand and pushed the tangled hair from her face. "What?"

"Are you in pain?"

Her brows furrowed, and she shifted slightly.

"Stay still," he said. "Wait until the medics check you out."

"My legs…" she whispered, panic lighting her face. "I can't move them."

TERROR SEIZED NINA. Her head was aching, but she couldn't feel her legs. "Slade, I can't move…"

"Shh, don't panic. The front end of the car is crunched," he said. "The rescue workers will have to cut us out."

Outside, sirens screeched, the fire truck roared to a stop, footsteps pounded on the asphalt and voices shouted.

Slade glanced up to see a firefighter and policeman kneeling and looking through his shattered window. "Are you two hurt?"

"We're trapped," Slade said.

The men exchanged concerned looks. "The ambulance is on its way."

Slade pulled Nina's hand in his and squeezed it between both of his. "Hang in there, Nina."

She clung to his hand, desperately holding on to her composure while she heard the men outside shouting orders. Noises sounded, more voices yelling. The ambulance arrived, the rescue workers manipulating the Jaws of Life, and someone shouted that a news crew had arrived.

The next hour blurred as the firemen worked to release them. Metal scraped, machinery ground and sawed through metal, jarring the car and her aching head and body.

Slade cradled her hand against his chest, kissed her palms and stroked her face, talking to her the entire time the firemen worked. His gruff voice helped calm her, and finally she heard voices murmuring they almost had them out.

Her breathing hitched as the metal gave way, and her legs were freed. Numbness had crept in, but pinpoints of pain stabbed her as feeling began to return.

"Nina?" Slade asked.

She massaged her leg with her hands. "My ankle hurts."

A small smile tilted his mouth. "That's actually good news."

Relief poured through her, but the medics insisted she shouldn't move.

"We have to board you until we transport you to the hospital and the doctors check you out."

She nodded, sucking in a sharp breath and closing her eyes as they secured her neck and body on the board and carried her to the ambulance. A camera flashed in her face, a half-dozen people scrambling around, and she tried to see Slade, but lost him in the commotion.

More voices drifted through the haze.

"My name is Sheriff Driscill," a male voice said. "What happened?"

"My brakes failed," Slade said. "Examine the SUV and see if they were tampered with."

Nina gripped the sides of the stretcher. Was it possible someone had tried to kill them?

FURY ROLLED THROUGH SLADE. He wanted to know why the hell his brakes had failed and, if there was foul play, who was responsible.

They both could have died.

Maybe that had been the plan....

"Why do you suspect foul play?" the sheriff asked.

"I'm a private investigator," Slade explained. "And I've been working a case."

Sheriff Driscill scratched his head. "What case?"

Slade explained about the investigation.

Driscill made some notes in a pad he pulled from his pocket. "I'll have a crime unit take a look."

Slade thanked him. "I'd like to ride to the hospital with Nina."

The sheriff took Slade's business card, then Slade joined the medics. His knee was throbbing, and he had a cut on his arm he'd let them take care of when they arrived at the hospital, but he had to make sure Nina was all right.

She opened her eyes when he climbed in

the back of the ambulance, and he perched on the stretcher across from her and cradled her hand in his.

"Slade?"

Dammit, he hated to see her beautiful face bruised. "Are you in pain?"

"My ankle and head hurt, but I'm okay." She licked her lips. "What about you?"

He shrugged. "I've had worse."

Her breathing hitched. "You said the brakes failed?"

He clenched his jaw. "Yes."

"You think they were tampered with?"

"I'd bet my life on it," Slade said bitterly. "And if whoever did this thought they'd scare me away or kill us, the only thing they did was piss me off."

She smiled, although she winced in pain, and he squeezed her hand. "It's going to be all right, Nina," he said softly. "Just rest. I'll take care of everything."

Protective instincts pulsed through him. He wanted to hold her, kiss her, remind himself that they were both alive.

He wanted to strangle the son of a bitch who'd tried to kill them.

The siren began to wail, the ambulance roared away and he vowed to get vengeance and find Nina's little girl.

THE NEXT TWENTY-FOUR hours became a fog of blurred memories in Nina's mind. The doctors and nurses treated her cuts and abrasions, wrapped her ankle, which thankfully wasn't broken but sprained, took X-rays, an MRI and a CAT scan and decided she was lucky.

But every bone in her body ached. And nightmares of careening off that bridge filled her restless sleep.

Other times, she saw Peyton standing a few feet away, so close she could almost touch her, but each time she reached out her fingers, her little girl slipped away.

She woke with tears on her cheeks, her chest hurting.

Slade sat beside her, looking rugged and angry, his clothes tattered from the accident, and a bruise discoloring his scarred cheek. But he'd stayed with her all night around the clock, and even exhausted, he was the most handsome man she'd ever seen.

"How are you feeling?" he asked in a gruff voice.

She pushed her hair from her face, wincing as she attempted to sit up. He yanked another pillow from the closet and eased it behind her back.

"Thanks." Glancing down, she realized the hospital gown had slipped off her shoulder, and she adjusted it, feeling naked and vulnerable.

"You didn't have to stay," she said.

His frown deepened. "The sheriff called. The brake lines to my SUV were definitely cut."

A small gasp escaped her. "So someone intentionally caused us to crash."

He nodded. "That means we must be getting close, that we've got someone worried."

"So you think Peyton might be alive?"

He was so quiet she didn't think he was going to answer. Finally, when he did, his tone was flat. "I don't know. But obviously someone knows what happened to her and doesn't want us to uncover the truth."

SLADE'S CELL PHONE buzzed, and he flipped the phone open. "Blackburn."

"This is Roan Waldorp, Mr. Blackburn. I want you to leave my family alone."

Slade frowned. "I'm conducting an investigation into a missing child, Mr. Waldorp, so I'm questioning everyone connected to the hospital fire eight years ago."

"I know exactly what you're doing. My wife suffered enough trauma back then, and I won't allow you to come to our home and upset her by implying that we did anything illegal."

"Mr. Waldorp," Slade cut in. "Who arranged for you to adopt that little girl?"

"That's none of your business. My wife and I lost a child, then were lucky enough to adopt another one. A perfect little girl and she's ours, so leave us alone."

He slammed down the phone, and Slade gritted his teeth. A perfect family. One the man didn't want disturbed.

"What was that about?" Nina asked.

"Waldorp warned me to stay out of his life."

Nina sucked in a harsh breath, and Slade punched in the number for GAI. While Nina had slept, he'd phoned to inform him of the accident—and the brakes being tampered with.

"Gage, it's Slade again."

"How's Nina?"

"Awake now, and feeling better, I think. But Waldorp was pissed that we'd questioned his wife about their adopted daughter. Can you ask Ben or Derrick to check into that adoption?"

"Sure. As a matter of fact, Derrick said that Brianna arranged a meeting with one of the social workers from the state adoption agency."

"I'll be there. Anything else?"

Gage made a sound of frustration. "I checked out the Hood family's alibis for the night of the fire. Two of William's buddies confirmed he was in a bar with them that night until midnight."

"His buddies could be lying for him."

"It's possible," Gage conceded. "Mrs. Hood's alibi holds up, as well. I found an article about the society party she attended, and phoned three of the people in attendance. They all corroborated her story."

"But she could have hired someone to kidnap the baby and paid for the adoption."

"True. But we have no proof yet."

"How about William's wife, Mitzi?"

"According to her father, she was home all night."

Like a father wouldn't lie to protect his daughter.

Another voice echoed in the room, and Gage paused, then spoke a second later. "Ben wants to talk to you about something he found." Gage transferred the call, and a second later, Camp's voice echoed over the line.

"Blackburn, I've been checking into Nash and the Hood family, digging up old phone records. It might not be anything, but Mr. Nash made several phone calls to a lawyer in

Sanctuary in the weeks before and after Nina gave birth."

Slade's suspicions rose. "Calls that could have indicated he was arranging an adoption?"

"That's what I was thinking. Do you want me to talk to the lawyer?"

"No, thanks. I'll pay him a visit. What's his name?"

"Stanford Mansfield." Camp paused, and Slade heard him pop his knuckles. "Blackburn, this is interesting, too. Mansfield's father and Nina's father attended college together. They also belong to the same Rotary club."

Slade stewed over the connection. A coincidence maybe, but if the men were friends, they might have exchanged favors.

"Check out his financials around that time period," Slade said. "See if Nash made any large withdrawals."

"I'm on it."

"Thanks. Good work." Slade disconnected the call and saw Nina watching him. She looked tired and pale, the bruises on her cheeks and arms more pronounced in the daylight.

"What's going on?"

Slade swallowed hard. He had to tell Nina

the truth—he'd promised her he would, no matter what he learned.

But how could he tell her that her father might have arranged for an adoption behind her back? That he might be responsible for taking away her child?

NINA NOTICED THE SUBTLE tension lining Slade's jaw. Something was wrong.

"Slade?"

He shifted. "I need to go question a lawyer named Stanford Mansfield."

Nina sensed he was avoiding her gaze. "What does he have to do with this?"

Slade hesitated. "There were several phone calls between him and your father around the time Peyton went missing."

"You think my father paid this lawyer to arrange for an adoption behind my back?"

Slade's eyes darkened. "I don't know, Nina. I'm just following the leads. That's why I want to talk to Mansfield."

She threw off the covers, searching for her clothes. "Let me get dressed. I'm going with you." But pain sliced through her ankle, and she winced and gripped the bed to keep from falling.

Slade caught her in one arm. "Whoa, you aren't going anywhere. You need to rest."

Nina angled her face toward him. "I can't just lie here in bed, not when we're getting so close." She pulled away, hobbled to the closet and dug out her clothes.

"Nina, please stay here and rest."

She ignored him and reached to untie the gown, but realized Slade was watching.

His gaze skated over her, and a tingle traveled up her spine. "Go ask the doctor for my release papers and let's get out of here."

"I can do this on my own," Slade said quietly. "You look—"

"As if I've been beaten up," Nina said with an eyebrow raise.

"Yes," he said tightly.

She offered him a smile. "I know. But so do you."

"I'm used to it," Slade said.

She laughed. "Maybe. But that's not the point. If this lawyer helped steal my baby from me, he needs to see me like this. And I want to tell him that I'm not giving up. Not now. Not ever."

REBECCA HAD TO DO something to make the man and woman like her. They stayed mad all the time, and if they were mad, they'd send her back to the orphanage.

She closed her book, *Pippi Longstocking,*

and stuffed it into her tote bag. Pippi was her favorite character in the whole wide world. She wanted to be just like her.

Mama Reese kept complaining about the kitchen floor being dirty. Rebecca would clean it. And if she used Pippi's way, she could do it fast before the old woman woke up.

Her snores echoed from the couch, and Rebecca found the dust mop and a pair of scissors. It took her almost twenty minutes to cut off the ends and divide it in two. Then she dragged the plastic bucket inside, pulled over a chair and climbed in it to reach the sink. She dumped dishsoap inside, then let water run in the bucket.

The handle was wobbly, and the bucket swung back and forth as she tried to climb down from the chair. Then the bucket slipped and water poured over the sides.

She started to yell out, but she couldn't wake Mama Reese. No, she had to clean up the mess.

Soapy water ran across the floor, and she skated across it, sloshing soap across the floor in her path. She nearly slipped twice, but grabbed the table edge, spun around and skated back the other way, zigzagging back and forth.

Suddenly the old woman shrieked. "What are you doing?"

Rebecca stopped and smiled. "Cleaning the floor for you."

But the old woman didn't smile back. She bared her teeth and bunched her hands into fists.

"Look at the mess you've made!" Mama Reese stormed toward her, jerked her arm so hard it hurt and shoved her into the chair.

Rebecca gripped the edge of the chair, her heart thudding. "I'm sorry…"

"You ruined my mop and now you made a big mess for me to clean up." The woman's fingernails dug into her arms. "I don't know what I'm going to do with you, you little brat. You're not worth the pitiful amount of money they give us every month."

Tears pricked Rebecca's eyes, then the woman jerked the mop pieces from her feet and dragged her toward the bedroom. Cursing beneath her breath, she threw open the closet door, shoved her inside then slammed the door.

"We're going to get rid of you," the woman yelled. "I don't want you here anymore!"

Rebecca reached for the doorknob, but the lock clicked in place and she was pitched into the dark. Tears burned her eyes and rolled down her cheeks as she pulled her knees to her chest, hugging them.

What would happen to her now? No one wanted her.…

Chapter Thirteen

Slade insisted they return to their houses and shower before confronting the lawyer. Nina was relieved to have some time to prepare herself for the visit.

If her father was connected… No, she couldn't believe that he would hurt her by deceiving her so ruthlessly.

Gage had dropped off a rental car, and they drove to Slade's place first since hers was closer to the lawyer's office.

"You own the house?" Nina asked.

"Yeah. It needs some work, but I liked the location," he said as he guided her up the steps to the porch and inside.

"It has charm," she said, admiring the two-story with the big front porch. "And the view of the mountains is spectacular. It's so private, too…"

"That was another plus," Slade said. "I like the solace."

She imagined the house with fresh white paint, flower boxes on the windowsills, a garden out back, and knew it would make a beautiful home once he finished renovations. She envisioned a passel of little children running around in the yard.

But Slade liked the peace and quiet—he wanted to be alone, not have a family. And she had to remember that.

As they stepped inside, she noted the sparse furnishings. A comfortable leather couch and throw rug, a big club chair, stereo, but no pictures on the walls or mantel.

Then she noticed the photograph of a young girl about ten and a brunette woman perched on the desk in the corner. It had to be his mother and sister.

"Do you need anything while I shower? Something to drink?"

"No, thanks, I'm fine. I'll just wait here." She sank onto his overstuffed sofa, and he stared at her for a long moment, then nodded. His boots pounded on the steps, and a second later, the shower water kicked on.

An image of Slade undressing flashed into her mind, and she closed her eyes and groaned. He was tall, broad-shouldered and, she imagined, deeply tanned and muscled beneath those clothes. She could almost see the soapy water beading on his skin, see his thick body hardening....

She jerked her eyes open, shocked at her train of thought. Good grief, she was not the lustful type. She was a schoolteacher. She'd been alone so long that she hadn't even thought about being with a man.

She'd been solely focused on surviving one day at a time. On school. On teaching. On holding on to faith when her faith had been crushed so many times.

Frustrated, she stood, walked over to the photograph and studied it. The little girl looked happy, the mother smiling, her arm curved protectively around her child.

Only their lives had fallen apart when the girl had become lost.

That was the reason Slade understood her anguish. He'd suffered his own.

Then she spotted a box of things he'd unpacked in the corner by the fireplace and glanced inside. Some plaques from the service, a medal for bravery.

Slade's footsteps sounded, the stairs squeaking as he descended. When he noticed her looking at his things, his jaw clenched.

"Are you ready?"

Nina nodded, but her palms felt sweaty at the sight of him fresh from the shower. His hair was still damp and tousled as if he'd just run the towel through it. And he hadn't buttoned the top button of his denim shirt, which revealed his golden-bronzed chest.

"Nina?" Something hot and sultry smoldered in his eyes, and her belly tickled.

But heat climbed her face as she realized he knew she'd been staring. The moment felt intimate. She had to distract herself, so she gestured toward the photograph.

"You were a war hero. That's impressive."

"Trust me, Nina, I was no hero."

"I don't believe you, Slade."

He gestured toward the scar on his cheek. "See that? I got it escaping while three of my men died saving me."

Anguish and guilt underscored his self-deprecating tone, raising her curiosity. He knew everything about her, all her deep, dark secrets, while she knew very little about him.

She gestured toward the picture. "Your sister was pretty. What happened to her?"

Any heat that had passed between them died, and his expression became closed. "She got mixed up with the wrong crowd, and ran away. Died. End of story."

His cell phone buzzed, abruptly ending the conversation, and he connected it as he gestured toward the door.

"Blackburn." He paused. "Yeah, okay. Thanks."

"Who was that?" Nina asked as they made their way to the sedan.

"Ben Camp again. I asked him to check into your father's financials around the time of the hospital fire."

Nina's pulse rocketed. "And?"

For a brief second, he hesitated as if he didn't want to admit what he'd learned.

"You promised not to keep things from me," she said.

He released a pent-up sigh and started the engine. "He found a large withdrawal from your father's personal account the week before you delivered Peyton."

Nina's stomach sank, and she turned to look out the window as he drove to her house. When they arrived, he strode around to help her from the car. "I'm sorry, Nina. We could be wrong about your father."

She fished for her keys and shook her head. "And you could be right. Daddy likes control. He obviously thought I wasn't mother material back then."

"As a father, he wanted the best for you," Slade said. "A bright future, college."

She frowned. "So you're defending him?"

"No, not at all. I'm just trying to get in his

head. Some men want to protect their kids no matter what. Even if they do make the wrong decisions."

She gritted her teeth. He'd described her father to a *T*.

Silently she limped to her bedroom, stripped and climbed in the shower. Battling tears, she stood beneath the shower massage, allowing the warm water to soothe her sore muscles. Her chest was bruised from the air bag, her legs battered from the dash and her face looked as if someone had taken a fist to it.

But her physical injuries didn't matter. Her heart was breaking.

If her father had paid someone to take Peyton away and had lied to her all these years, she would never forgive him.

WHILE NINA SHOWERED, Slade distracted himself from thinking about her being naked and wet by searching the computer for background information on the lawyer.

As a teenager, Mansfield had hidden behind his daddy's money. Was he hiding behind money now?

He found several articles on the lawyer, cases he'd handled, but nothing specific to suggest illegal behavior.

Still, judging from the pricey area where he lived, and his Mercedes, he was rolling in the bucks. And none of the cases Slade noted were impressive enough to make him wealthy. He phoned to verify that the lawyer was in his office, and learned he was working at home for the day.

Nina emerged, looking vulnerable and soft and so damn pretty that something stirred inside him. He knew she was anxious about her father and hoped like hell he hadn't deceived her all these years.

He drove them to Mansfield's, a ten-acre estate on the outskirts of town on the river. "Looks like Mansfield has done well for himself."

The troubled expression on her face indicated she understood his implications. That she knew her father might have padded the man's wallet.

"Are you sure you're up to this?" Slade asked.

Nina nodded. "Yes. We've come this far. I'm not backing down now."

Slade traced a thumb over her wrist, his body instantly reacting to the warmth of her skin. "Not even after that attempt on our lives?"

"Like you said, if whoever did this thought

he scared me off, he's wrong. He only made me more determined that I'm right, that Peyton is out there somewhere, that she's alive."

Slade refused to comment. At this point, he knew something had happened eight years ago that somebody would kill to keep quiet, and he wanted the whole story now.

Her ankle was still slightly swollen, and she had to lean on Slade as they walked to the door. Her injuries only reminded him that they had nearly died the night before, raising his protective instincts. He had the insane urge to whisk her away to bed and protect her from the danger, and whatever they learned.

But she gave him a brave smile, and he punched the doorbell instead. The river gurgled and splashed over rocks behind Mansfield's property, and Slade noted tennis courts to the side, then heard the sound of a match being played on the courts.

So much for Mansfield working at home.

A maid greeted them at the door. "May I help you?"

"We're here to see Mr. Mansfield."

"He's busy at the moment. Can I make an appointment for you?"

Slade produced his ID. "No. We have urgent business. We need to see him now."

A nervous expression flitted across her face, but she gestured for them to follow. "He's having a tennis lesson," she said. "He won't like being disturbed."

"He'll get over it," Slade muttered sarcastically.

Nina leaned on him again, and they followed the maid through the house to a patio overlooking the tennis courts.

Mansfield glanced up and saw him, and missed his shot. The trainer said something to him, then Mansfield motioned that the lesson was over, leaned his racket against the fence and strode toward them, mopping his face with a towel.

His eyes narrowed on Nina as if he recognized her and knew the reason for their visit.

The maid offered an apologetic look. "They insisted it was important, Mr. Mansfield."

Mansfield gestured for her to go inside, sank into a patio chair with a curse then took a long drink from his water bottle. "What the hell do you two want?"

"You know who we are?" Slade asked.

The man wiped his mouth with the back of his hand. "Yes. I saw the news article about your accident this morning in the paper. You're a P.I." He crooked a thumb toward

Nina, his breathing labored from the exertion of his tennis lesson. "And everyone in town knows you, Miss Nash."

Anger pulsed inside Slade at the man's abrasive attitude. "I have some questions for you, Mansfield."

Mansfield wiped sweat from his neck with the towel. "You should be asking her the questions. Like why she keeps stirring up trouble."

"If she's stirring up trouble by asking questions, that means someone is keeping secrets." Slade gripped the man's collar. "In fact, some bastard tried to kill her—and me—last night. Was that bastard you, Mansfield?"

"Take your hands off me, Mr. Blackburn," Mansfield said, his eyes fuming.

"You know," Slade said, "for a bunch of innocent people, you and everyone I've talked to certainly are acting defensive."

"Go to hell," Mansfield spat out.

"I've already been there." Nina gestured toward the bruises on her face and arms. "Both physically and mentally."

Slade shoved him back into the chair. "Listen, Mansfield, I know for a fact that you and Nina's father had several phone conversations around the time her baby disappeared. I also know that Mr. Nash made a sizeable withdrawal, as well. My guess is that Nash paid you to arrange an adoption for her baby."

Mansfield released a withering sigh. "Miss Nash, your father approached me about arranging an adoption, but later he phoned me and claimed that you refused to sign the papers."

"That's true," Nina said.

"But he didn't give up, did he?" Slade pressed.

Mansfield drummed his fingers on the table. "He was persistent," Mansfield said. "He thought eventually Miss Nash would agree, but then she delivered the baby prematurely and the fire occurred that night, and the baby died, so the point became moot."

"So my father didn't pay you to find a family for my baby?" Nina asked.

His expression turned chilly. "No."

"What about the Waldorp's adoption?" Slade said. "Did you handle it?"

"Whether I did or did not is none of your business." Mansfield stood and gestured toward the door. "Adoptions are sealed and confidential, and I'm bound by attorney-client privilege. I could be disbarred if I shared any information about them."

"Being disbarred will be the least of your

problems if you were complicit in kidnapping and arranging a phony adoption." Slade squared his shoulders. "I'll see that you rot in jail, and your career will be over."

NINA STRUGGLED TO BELIEVE in her father's innocence as they left the lawyer's house and drove to meet Brianna McKinney and the social worker at the adoption agency.

Brianna greeted them with a genuine smile, putting Nina immediately at ease. "I've heard about your ordeal, Nina, and I can't imagine what you've been through. My adopted son was kidnapped a few months ago, and it was the most harrowing experience of my life."

Nina recalled the story in the paper about the abduction. "I read about you," Nina said. "That case led to the arrests regarding the hospital fire and explosion."

Brianna nodded, and led her and Slade into an office where an auburn-haired woman with freckles sat, studying a file.

"Miriam," Brianna said, "this is Slade Blackburn of GAI, and Nina Nash, the woman I told you about." She gestured toward her and Slade. "This is Miriam Sheppard. She works with the state adoption agency."

They exchanged pleasantries, then Slade spoke. "Miss Sheppard, we're looking into the possibility that Nina's baby was kidnapped, then adopted." He explained the Hoods' and her father's reactions to her pregnancy. "We think Stanford Mansfield might have been paid to arrange the adoption. And it's possible that Gwen and Roan Waldorp took the child. They have an adopted daughter the same age as Nina's child."

"You know adoption records are sealed," Miriam said.

"Please," Nina begged. "Just tell us what you know."

Miriam glanced at Brianna warily then sighed. "All I can tell you, and this is under the table, is that the Waldorp adoption was not a state adoption."

"Meaning it was a private adoption?" Slade asked.

She nodded in confirmation.

"Do you have records of a premature baby being adopted around that time?" Slade asked. "And could that child have been adopted by the Waldorps?"

Miriam spoke quietly. "I have no record of preemie adoptions, or suggestions that the Waldorps have your child, but I'll dig deeper. She could have ended up in foster care."

"My poor little girl," Nina said in a pained

whisper. "What if no one adopted her and she's lost in the system?"

Miriam smiled for the first time since they'd entered. "It's possible. I'll search and see if I find a child in foster care who matches that description."

Hope budded in Nina's chest. But it was a long shot. For all she knew, a family had adopted her. If so, she only prayed that they loved her.

But that nagging sensation clawed at her, and she closed her eyes. She could hear her little girl crying again.

She needed her.

Nina would find her no matter what.

SLADE HATED THE DISCOMFORT on Nina's face, but if Peyton was in foster care, it might be easier to track her down than if she had been adopted. But the thought of the little handi-capped girl being shuffled from one place to another, knowing she might have suffered God knew what, ripped at his gut.

He knew firsthand what foster care was like. Knew that some people could be loving, but that other times, they could be cruel.

His cell phone buzzed, and he excused him-self to answer it. "Slade Blackburn."

"Mr. Blackburn," a woman's voice whispered. "This is Paula Emery."

Slade tensed. "Yes?"

A tension-filled minute stretched between them. Slade thought he heard shuffling, then running. "Mrs. Emery?"

"I have to see you," she cried. "Roan Waldorp called here a few minutes ago having a fit. I think I may know who kidnapped Nina Nash's child."

He sucked in a sharp breath. "The Waldorps?"

"Not over the phone," she whispered. "Meet me at Caleb's Cabins off Old Canyon Road. The cabin at the end of the road."

A man's voice sounded in the background, and the woman's breath quickened. "I can't talk now. I have to go. Just meet me."

The line went dead, and Slade rushed back in to get Nina. Mrs. Emery sounded scared, nervous.

Did she really know who had kidnapped Peyton, or was this some kind of trap?

Chapter Fourteen

Slade stepped back into the room. "Nina, we need to go. We might have a lead."

Hope brightened her face, and she stood, although her ankle gave way and she gripped his arm to steady herself.

"I can drop you at the agency if you want," he offered.

"No. I'm going with you." She clung to his arm and he helped her out to the rental car. "What happened?" she asked as she fastened her seat belt.

Slade started the engine. "That was Dr. Emery's wife. She said Gwen's husband called, frantic about our visit. Then she claimed she has information about Peyton."

"Oh, my God…" Nina's eyes filled with tears.

"I hope she's telling the truth, Nina," he said, feeling the need to caution her. "But we have to be careful. This could be a trap."

"A trap?"

He squeezed her hand. "Remember, someone tried to kill us already."

"But why would Mrs. Emery want to hurt us?"

"To protect her husband," Slade said matter-of-factly.

Nina thumbed a strand of hair from her cheek and slowly nodded.

A thunderstorm rumbled on the horizon, the clouds thickening as they climbed the mountain toward the rental cabins. Traffic thinned, a single car or truck passing as night fell. The wind whipped leaves from the trees, the temperature dropping, the area becoming more isolated and dense with woods.

Slade checked the rearview mirror a dozen times to make certain no one was following. Lights from an oncoming truck nearly blinded him as he rounded a curve, then a deer raced across the road. The truck's brakes squealed as he swerved to avoid it, and Slade skimmed the side of the road to avoid hitting the truck.

His lights flickered down the embankment, and he caught sight of a car that had nose-dived into the small ravine. The truck raced on, oblivious.

"Damn. There's a car off the road down

there," Slade said, righting his vehicle and pulling a few feet ahead to an overhang. "Let me see if anyone is hurt inside."

Nina nodded, and he jumped out. "Lock the door. And if anyone approaches, honk the horn." He didn't wait on a reply. He raced down the embankment, dirt and rocks skidding beneath his boots.

He skated over the rocks but his foot slipped, and he grabbed a tree limb to keep from falling. Cursing, he climbed over a tree stump, and mangled limbs scattered across the terrain from a past storm then placed his hand on the car. It was still warm.

The front end was crunched into the ravine, the windows shattered, the sides dented, and the mirror on the driver's side had been ripped off.

Pushing through the briars and weeds, he looked inside the window at the driver's seat. A body was plastered against the seat, half hidden by the air bag. He used his pocketknife to rip it away, then saw the woman's bloody face. Her skin was ashen, her chest heaving for air.

"Miss, my name is Slade Blackburn. I'll call an ambulance."

"Wait…" she rasped. "She did this…"

"She?" He frowned and tilted her face to see her eyes. "What are you talking about?"

"I called you," she choked out.

Cold fear gripped Slade's belly. "You're Dr. Emery's wife?"

Her body jerked and convulsed, another pain-filled choked sound erupting from her.

"Ye-es," she whispered. "Carrie Poole, nurse…affair with my husband. She…stole the baby."

Slade's heart pounded. He had to get help. "I'm going to call an ambulance."

But suddenly the woman rasped another sound, gripped her chest and panic filled her eyes.

Then she slumped back in the seat, her eyes glazed over and she stopped breathing.

NINA WONDERED WHAT WAS taking so long. Was someone in the car? Maybe hurt…

Suddenly, a shot blasted the front window of the car, and she ducked. Another shot hit the front bumper and pinged off, and she screamed.

Where was the shooter? In the woods? Had he hit Slade?

Panic flooded her. No, Slade couldn't be hurt….

Another shot echoed from the other side,

and she heard Slade shouting, "Stay down, Nina!"

She covered her head with her arms and did as he said, while more gunfire exploded around her. Outside the car, footsteps crunched gravel, thunder rumbled then she heard someone scrambling near the passenger door.

Was it the shooter?

Rain began to splatter the windshield, and the door lock clicked then the door swung open.

Nina sighed in relief when she spotted Slade sliding into the seat. "Are you all right?"

"Yes. What about you?"

Another shot pelted the passenger side this time, and he twisted the key in the ignition, punched the accelerator and took off. "Hang on," he shouted.

Nina refastened her seat belt but crouched low as he raced around the curve. He shoved his cell phone toward her.

"Call the sheriff, tell them I found Emery's wife's car crashed." He paused and gave her a troubled look. "And tell him to send the coroner. She's dead."

"Oh, my God…" She started punching in numbers while he maneuvered the curves. "What happened?"

"I don't know," Slade said. "But if that

shooter was any indication, she was murdered."

Nina gasped. "She was killed because she was going to talk to me."

Slade pulled her hand into his lap. "This is not your fault, Nina. So don't even go there. For all we know, Mrs. Emery knew who the kidnapper was all along and remained quiet all these years."

A deep-seated trembling overcame Nina, and she gripped his hand tighter. "Did you see the shooter?" she whispered.

Slade shook his head, then veered onto a dirt side road that wound along the creek. Nina spotted the sign for the rental cabins, and realized they were still headed to Emery's cabin.

"What did she say?" Nina asked.

"She claimed her husband and Carrie had an affair."

"Carrie and Dr. Emery?" Nina frowned. "That doesn't seem likely."

Slade shrugged. "Maybe, maybe not. But if Emery didn't know about the kidnapping, and Carrie was responsible for killing his wife, she may be going after him next."

NINA'S HANDS WERE trembling so hard that Slade took the phone. "This is Slade Blackburn of GAI." He relayed what had happened and asked for an ambulance.

"I'm going to check out the doctor's cabin now."

"I'll send someone up there to comb the woods ASAP. Call me if you need backup." Sheriff Driscill paused. "And, Blackburn, remember, you're not a cop. You don't have a warrant so keep it within the law."

Slade gritted his teeth. "Yeah, right." He ended the call with a curse. To hell with the law.

He and Nina had been nearly killed twice. Mrs. Emery was dead.

And someone didn't want them to find out what had happened to Peyton Nash.

He'd do whatever it took to find the truth now. Even if he had to risk his reputation, his job and his life to do so.

He swerved around a pothole, gravel spewing from the tires as he ground his way across the dirt road. Rain pounded the roof of the car, the thunder growing louder, and he slowed slightly, creeping past several cabins until he reached the hollow. A lone cabin sat atop the hill, a small sedan parked outside.

A streak of lightning shot across the sky, illuminating the dark interior of the cabin, and he scanned the perimeter. No lights on inside or outside.

Was anyone home? Or could the shooter be hiding out here?

No. On foot, he couldn't have woven through the woods that quickly.

He threw the car into Park and glanced at Nina. "Stay here with the doors locked. I'll check out the cabin and see if anyone's here."

Nina grabbed his hand. "Slade…"

"Yeah?"

"Be careful." Her lower lip quivered. "Please."

Her eyes were big, beautiful pools of color, filled with fear. Fear for him.

Something deep and untamed moved inside him. Arousal? Need? Hunger?

That and emotions he had never felt or thought he would feel for a woman. God, he didn't want to lose her.…

Inhaling a deep breath, he cupped her face in his hands. "I will. Stay put and if you hear or see anyone, hit the horn like I told you earlier."

Slade kissed her deeply, tenderly, urgently. Desire surged through him along with protective instincts and the need to tell her that he cared for her.

No… Too scary.

A dog barked somewhere in the distance, and reality sucker punched him. So he pulled away.

"Hurry," Nina whispered.

He nodded, then opened the door, slid outside and crept up to the house. Rain pelted him, and he scanned the land and exterior, then peered in through the front window. Although the house was dark, and he didn't detect movement, a noise jarred him.

A soft pounding? A knock?

He couldn't quite tell, so he crept to the side of the house, checking the windows there, searching for one that might be open. A deck had been built onto the back, and he padded up the steps, then jiggled the back door.

The noise sounded again. A knocking sound, maybe a fist or a chair? Then another sound…a moan.

His pulse spiked. Someone was inside, someone hurt.

He removed his wallet, removed the small lockpick he kept stored inside, jammed it in the lock and jimmied it open. The scent of coffee and something acrid filled the air, and he frowned and inched inside, keeping his gun at the ready.

Then he heard the moan again, a low,

keening sound of pain, and he moved forward, listening for other sounds as he inched through the kitchen into the small hallway leading to the living room. But his foot hit something, and he realized a chair was overturned.

The metallic scent of blood assaulted him, and he glanced down and found a woman lying on the floor. She had one hand wrapped around the chair, either trying to pull herself up or banging it to attract his attention.

"Help me," she whispered in a choked cry.

Slade knelt beside her and checked her pulse. Low but thready. The woman was Carrie Poole, the nurse from the hospital. Blood soaked her blouse, and she tried to raise a trembling hand to reach for him.

But it fell limply to her side, she gasped for a breath and her body convulsed.

NINA HEARD A NOISE NEAR the house, and panic set in. What was taking Slade so long?

Was he all right?

Her heart was pounding so loudly she could almost hear the blood roaring in her ears. She just couldn't sit here. She had to do something.

Then a car raced up the drive, a black Mercedes. Dr. Emery's.

Anxiety choked her, and for a moment, fear. What if Dr. Emery had known what Carrie had done?

But his face looked panicked as he jumped out and ran up to the sedan. The rain was starting to die down, but rivulets trickled down his cheeks as he pounded on the door.

"Nina, what are you doing here?" He frantically pulled at the door. "Open up. Have you seen my wife?"

Nina tensed and gripped the door handle. He didn't know about his wife's accident… that she was dead…

He threw up his hands, his face filled with fear. "Nina, open up, tell me what's going on."

Nina chewed her bottom lip, but opened the car door. If Carrie was inside, she might have laid a trap for the doctor. And Slade might have walked into it, meaning he needed help.

"My wife phoned, frantic," Dr. Emery said. "She claimed she knew who took your baby, that she was scared, for me to meet her here."

Nina inhaled a sharp breath. "I know…she called me, too."

His eyes raked over her, then fell to the empty driver's seat. "Did that P.I. come with you?"

Nina nodded. "He went inside to see if you were there. He thought you might be in danger..." Her voice cracked. "Dr. Emery, I don't know how to tell you this, but we found your wife's car crashed down the road. She didn't make it."

His eyes went flat, and suddenly he gripped her arm. "I know."

Nina stared at him in horror as he yanked her from the car and jammed a gun in her side.

Chapter Fifteen

Slade started to punch 9-1-1, but Carrie grabbed his arm. "I didn't do it…"

"Do what?" Slade asked.

"Didn't have an affair with…Dr. Emery…" Carrie gasped. "And I didn't kidnap the baby…"

"Then who did?" Slade asked.

"Mrs. Emery said I did…that I stole babies for him because I was sleeping with him…" Tears leaked down her pale cheeks as she struggled for a breath. "That's not true…"

Slade stroked her arm to calm her. "Carrie, do you know what happened to the Nash baby?"

"Adopted…I overheard doctor on the phone yesterday…" Her breathing grew labored, and Slade's jaw hardened.

Dammit. He wanted to know more but he couldn't let the woman die.

He punched in 9-1-1 and asked for an

ambulance and the sheriff, but suddenly the door squeaked open and footsteps shuffled in the front room. Alarm shot through him, then Nina's voice called his name.

"Slade?"

He glanced up and saw Nina in the shadow of the doorway, and his blood went cold.

Dr. Emery was standing behind her with a gun aimed at her head.

Nina was trembling so badly her knees were knocking. Carrie Poole lay on the floor, her chest soaked in blood, her breathing labored.

Had Dr. Emery shot her? Was he going to kill all of them?

Slade's eyes settled on her.

"Put your gun on the floor. Slowly," Dr. Emery said in an icy tone. "And if you make any sudden moves, I'll kill her."

"You son of a bitch," Slade growled.

Dr. Emery jerked her arm, and Slade raised his hands in surrender. "All right. Just don't hurt her." Slowly, he lowered his gun hand and placed the piece on the floor.

"Now move away from it," Dr. Emery ordered.

"Why are you doing this?" Nina whispered

as Slade inched closer toward them. "You're supposed to save lives, not take them."

Dr. Emery's fingers dug into her arm. "I do save lives. I saved your baby's, didn't I?"

"But you told me she died in that fire," Nina said bitterly. "That's not true, is it?"

"Why couldn't you just move on and forget about her?" Dr. Emery growled. "That's what your father wanted. What everyone wanted."

Slade cleared his throat. "What did you do to Peyton, Emery?"

"You two ask too many damn questions. My wife…" His voice cracked. "She had to die because of you."

Carrie groaned from the floor, and the doctor jerked Nina sideways. "And now she's going to die, too, and it's all your fault."

"My fault," Nina said in a ragged whisper. "You're crazy. I'm just a mother who wants to know what happened to her child."

"What did you do?" Slade asked in a level tone. "Is Peyton still alive?"

"I have no idea where that child is now," Dr. Emery said sharply. "I arranged for her to go to a good home, a home with two parents, two who would know how to raise a handicapped child."

"How could you be so cruel?" Nina said.

"I loved my baby. I wouldn't have cared if she had problems. I would have taken care of her—"

"You were too young to have a child," Dr. Emery snapped. "Even your father wanted you to give up the baby."

Nina's lungs tightened so painfully she couldn't breathe. "Did my father have something to do with this?"

The doctor shook his head. "No, but he was happy the child was gone. He wanted you to grow up, move on." He shook her again, and she felt the cold metal of the barrel against her temple. "But you refused to let it go."

"Because my baby is out there and she needs me," Nina argued.

"No, she doesn't. She's better off, just like the others."

A sick feeling swept over Nina.

Slade balled his hands into fists. "What others?"

Sweat trickled down the side of the doctor's face. "The other little whores who got knocked up without being married."

Nina couldn't believe what she was hearing.

"So what do you plan to do, Emery? Kill all of us? You can't believe that you'll get away with it?"

The doctor's hand jerked as he frantically looked around the room. Then a sinister laugh escaped him. "Hell, I'll make it look like Nina killed you both. She had a breakdown before. It won't be hard to make it look like she had another."

He waved the gun toward Slade. "Now get down on your knees."

Nina's heart started racing. She couldn't die, not knowing Peyton had survived.

She had to fight to stay alive so she could find her.

SLADE SAW THE WHEELS turning in Nina's mind. She didn't intend to give up.

But he didn't want her to do anything stupid that could get her killed. Dammit, he had to save her. Save both of them.

Where was that damn ambulance? And the sheriff?

"I've already phoned the sheriff. And all my people at GAI are on the case, Emery," Slade said calmly. "There's no use in taking any more lives."

"Shut up."

"Killing us will only add more to your sentence," Slade continued. "But if you turn yourself in, you might be able to swing some kind of deal."

"Deal?" Emery barked. "My career, my life will be over."

"Your life will be over anyway," Slade said. "The sheriff is going to be here any moment."

"You're bluffing," Emery bit out.

Slade shrugged. "I called when I found Carrie."

Slade glanced at Nina and saw her eyes flickering sideways toward the fireplace. A fire poker leaned against the brick hearth, and he sensed the direction of her thoughts. He tried to signal her not to risk it, but a siren echoed in the distance, Emery jerked his head toward the door in shock and Nina shoved him away from her.

She wasn't strong enough though, and Emery pistol-whipped her across the face. She screamed and flew backward from the impact, then landed against the hearth with a groan.

Slade cursed and lunged toward the doctor, but the gun went off. The bullet skimmed his arm, and he ducked sideways and rammed his head into the man's stomach.

Emery grunted, and they fell to the floor, struggling for the gun. Another shot pinged into the ceiling, sending plaster raining down. Slade shoved Emery's head against the wall, clawing at Emery's fingers to force him to release his hold on the weapon. Emery kneed him, and he flipped him sideways, then the gun fired another bullet and he heard Nina scream.

Fear shot through him. Had she been shot?

The second he took to look gave Emery an advantage, and he rolled Slade to his back. Determination seized Slade, and he karate-chopped Emery's arm. The blow made Emery yelp and the gun fell to the floor beside them.

Emery's eyes went wild with panic and rage. The siren wailed closer. Nina moaned and tried to get up from the hearth, staggering.

Slade thought of the pain she'd suffered all these years, of her lost little girl, of Emery lying to her and making her think she was crazy, and cold fury empowered him.

He slammed his fist into Emery's face and sent his head rolling back. Another punch and the man fell to his back, but his hand slid around the gun on the floor beside them. Slade lunged for it, but Nina had grabbed the fire poker and swung it down. The poker caught Emery's arm above the wrist, and the bone snapped.

Emery yelped in pain, dropped the gun and Slade grabbed it then stood.

"You're going to jail, Emery," Slade snarled.

His breath gushed out as he reached for Nina. She fell into his arms, trembling and crying, and he kissed her hair and hugged her to him.

THE NEXT FEW HOURS blurred for Nina. The ambulance and sheriff arrived, along with a crime unit, and they rushed an unconscious Carrie to the hospital. Another team raced up and checked her head for injuries, but she assured them she was fine, then they treated Slade where his arm had been grazed by the bullet.

Sheriff Driscill arrested Dr. Emery, but he refused to talk, insisting that he wanted a lawyer. The medics splinted his arm, then loaded him in the ambulance.

Slade filled the sheriff in on everything that had happened.

"So Emery killed his wife and shot Carrie because they found out what he was doing and threatened to tell?" Sheriff Driscill asked.

"That was my impression," Slade said. "Maybe you can force more information from the doctor."

The sheriff turned to Nina. "And he admitted that he kidnapped your baby?"

"He confirmed that he arranged an adoption," Nina answered.

"I think Stanford Mansfield was involved in the deal," Slade said.

"I'll have him picked up," the sheriff said. "And I'll obtain warrants to subpoena Emery's files."

"Good," Slade said. "Let me know when you bring Mansfield in. I want to be there when you interrogate him."

Driscill agreed then headed to the ambulance to ride with Emery.

Slade cupped Nina's elbow in his hand. "Are you all right?"

She nodded, although she felt numb inside. For so long she'd sensed that her daughter hadn't died in that fire and now to have that fact confirmed created a mixture of emotions. Relief that she'd survived. Hope that she might find her. Anger over the years they'd lost together. Anxiety over where she was and who had been caring for her.

Fear that she still might never find her.

Slade coaxed her back to the car, helped her inside, and she fastened her seat belt. When he settled inside, he gave her a concerned look, then started the engine and drove away from the blinding lights of the police cruiser and the crime scene they'd just been a part of.

"I know a thousand things are going through your mind right now," Slade said gruffly.

She gave a small, sardonic laugh. "Since when did you become a mind reader?"

He chuckled. "Because they're going through my mind, as well."

Could he really understand? No… No one could…

"I guess I should be glad to have answers," she finally said. "And I am. But…"

"But you want to know more?"

"Yes," she said softly. She turned to look out the window, and focused on the rain dripping from the branches, heard the slush of water as the tires rolled over wet pavement. An image of her and her daughter singing in the rain flashed into her mind, and fresh pain rocked through her. She could almost hear Peyton's voice again singing in a low tone.

"Emery indicated that he'd arranged for other babies to be adopted," Slade said, jarring her from her fantasies. "My guess is, the adoptions were all private and he was paid well, so I intend to have GAI study his financials and see if they connect with Mansfield's."

Hope bloomed in her chest like a rainbow

after a storm. Slade was on her side now. She wasn't alone.

There was still a chance that she could find Peyton.

She closed her eyes and said a silent prayer. And if Peyton didn't need her, if she'd found another mother, somehow she'd find peace in the lies and betrayal she'd suffered. After all, a mother's love meant being unselfish.

The only thing that mattered was that her daughter was safe and happy.

REBECCA SAT HUNCHED on the floor, her knees to her chest, her arms wrapped around herself, rocking back and forth, back and forth.

How long had she been in this dark closet? Were they ever going to come back?

She had to stay strong. Be tough. Not be a crybaby. She pictured Mary Poppins in her mind and heard her sing, so she joined in in a soft whisper.

Suddenly footsteps pounded in the bedroom. She held her breath at the stench of cigarette smoke seeping through the crack in the door. Then the door opened, and Daddy Reese grabbed her by the wrists and dragged her toward the kitchen. Her eyes hurt from the sudden, blinding light.

"We're getting rid of you now," he bellowed. "I can't stand it anymore."

She bit her lip so as not to cry as he tossed her into the kitchen, and she fell on the floor. Her chest heaved.

What did he mean? What were they going to do to her?

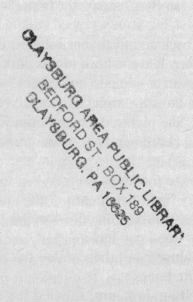

Chapter Sixteen

Nina suddenly doubled over as she entered her house, a sharp pain wrenching her heart. Something was wrong… She felt it deep in her bones.

Slade gripped her arm. "Nina, what is it?"

She closed her eyes and inhaled deeply, forcing herself to take slow breaths as the therapist had taught her years ago. One, two, three…breathe through the pain…

Slade suddenly swung her up into his arms and carried her toward her bedroom, then into the bath. "You should have let the medics admit you to the hospital."

"No…" Nina whispered. "It's Peyton… Something's wrong, Slade. Something's happening to her. I can feel it."

Slade tensed, but then pulled her into his arms. "Oh, honey…"

She fell against him, inhaled his deeply

masculine scent and clung to his strong arms. Slade had stayed with her, had protected her, had fought to find her child when everyone else had insisted she was crazy.

She needed him now. Needed him to hold her until she could pull herself together. Until she could find her daughter.

He cradled her against him, then gestured toward the tub. "I'll run you a hot bath, then fix you a drink. That will help you sleep."

She nodded, although sleep was the last thing on her mind. Sleep would bring the nightmares, the waking up to the emptiness, the lonely bed, the dark…

But she felt gritty with dirt and sweat, and needed the stench of the doctor off her skin, so she nodded, and he eased her to the floor. A numbness settled over her as Slade ran the bathwater, a coping mechanism to handle the shock of all that happened. But her mind kept replaying the past few hours.

Mrs. Emery had died. Carrie was in the hospital. The doctor she'd once trusted had shoved a gun at her head.

Slade sat on the edge of the tub and dumped in the bath salts, then brushed her hair back from her cheek. "I'll be downstairs if you need me."

"Thank you," she said softly.

For a moment, he simply stared at her, the tension between them palpable, the scent of his body filling the room and making her think crazy things.

Things like she wanted to ask him to join her in the bath. To make love to her.

As if he sensed that need and was sending her a silent message, he turned and walked out the door. Tears pricked her eyes as she undressed and climbed into the bath. Was she just a case to him, or could he possibly care?

He'd been so gentle earlier that she'd felt a connection with him. A connection that went deep. A connection that she didn't want to lose…

A connection that terrified her because she not only wanted him, but also needed him.

SLADE DRAGGED HIMSELF away from the bathroom when he really wanted to go inside, slowly remove Nina's clothes, climb in the bath with her and soap her delicate skin, then stroke her body until she groaned his name in oblivion.

The fact that she was struggling with her feelings over all that happened only endeared her to him. The fact that she'd fought so hard to find her daughter and to save herself and him stirred his admiration…and lust.

But there were more answers he needed to find. Not just for Nina but for himself.

He didn't even know her daughter, but he found himself worrying about her. Wondering how she'd survived. If she was safe and loved.

If someone had taken care of her needs.

Or if her handicaps had caused couples to reject her.

The thought of that made anger rail.

He'd wanted to kill Emery for hurting Nina and depriving her of her child. And of depriving the little girl of her birth mother.

Nina might have been young, but she would never have abandoned her daughter. She would have done everything humanly possible to see that she received the help she needed to thrive.

He heard a splash of water, and envisioned Nina naked, her creamy skin dotted with bubbles, and his body hardened.

He had to get a grip. He still had work to do. They had to break Emery. Interrogate Mansfield.

Forcing the mental picture of Nina naked from his mind, he phoned Gage to fill him in.

"I'll pass the info on to Derrick and

Brianna," Gage said. "See if they found a lead with the foster child angle."

"And I'll follow up with Driscill and Carrie Poole. Maybe she knows more than she's telling."

Gage grunted. "I'll be glad to finally nail that sleazebag Mansfield."

"You have history?" Slade asked.

"You could say that," Gage said. "He stood by and watched while a crime happened one night, but he got off scot-free."

It sounded personal, but if Gage wanted to share details he would. "How's Nina?" Gage asked.

Slade's throat felt dry as she slowly descended the stairs. A thin satin robe floated over her curves and made him wonder what she wore beneath it. "Hanging in there. I have to go."

He closed the phone, reminding himself that Nina was a client, and vulnerable.

But the sultry look in her eyes sent his pulse skyrocketing. The bruises from their earlier accident were still dark and purple, and the image of Emery shoving that gun at her head assaulted him, sending fear straight to his heart.

"Nina?" he said gruffly.

"I can't sleep," she whispered hoarsely. "I don't want to be alone, Slade."

Every professional instinct warned him to back off. Every self-preservation instinct ordered him to run like hell.

But the tearstains on her cheeks made his stomach knot. And the creamy cleavage that appeared where her robe fell open made his body harden and need surge in his loins.

"Go to bed," he said, making a last-ditch effort to do the right thing.

She reached out her hand. "Not alone. Not tonight."

"Nina…"

"Don't I deserve one night of pleasure?"

"Yes. Of course you do." Slade gripped his hands by his sides to keep from reaching for her, but his body betrayed him by aching for her, and he lost the battle with his conscience.

Nina was the bravest woman he'd ever met. Far stronger than he was. And he wanted to assuage her pain, to have her in his arms and bed.

So he took her hand and followed her up the steps.

NINA COULDN'T BELIEVE she was being so bold, but the hungry look in Slade's eyes when she'd descended the stairs had sparked her courage. His sultry eyes and mouth aroused her to the point of desperation.

She was tired of being alone. Of shutting herself off from others because she was afraid of loving and losing again.

Not that Slade would promise anything more than tonight.

But she didn't care. She still wanted one night in his bed, in his arms, with his lips and mouth and hands touching her intimately.

"Nina…" he said gruffly.

She offered him her most seductive smile, and his jaw clamped as if he was reining in his control.

Control be damned. She'd kept an ironclad leash on herself for years.

Not anymore. She was tired of the pain, of waiting for tomorrow.

"Nina, we shouldn't do this," Slade said in a husky voice. "You're vulnerable."

Her confidence slipped a notch. "You don't want me, Slade?"

His shoulders drew back as his gaze raked over her, and she noticed the thick bulge in his jeans. His breath quickened at her perusal, and a bead of perspiration dotted his forehead. "Yes, I want you," he said in a voice laden with sexual innuendo. "But—"

She pressed her finger to his lips to shush him. "But nothing. We almost died tonight."

His look darkened, anger radiating from him. "I know, dammit." He stepped toward her, then lifted his hand and stroked her hair from her face.

It was such a tender gesture that her heart swelled with affection, and her body throbbed with longing.

Heaven help her, she was falling in love with him. He could be so tough, so bold... so gentle, that arousal flooded her. Her body tingled, her nipples ached, between her thighs grew moist.

"You deserve more than a broken man like me," he said gruffly. "I'm scarred, inside and out."

"I'm scarred, too," she said softly.

A growl left his throat. "Nina, you're the strongest, most courageous, most beautiful woman I've ever met."

She slid her hand to the back of his neck to urge him toward her. "Then kiss me, dammit."

Slade chuckled, but the heat in his eyes intensified, then he dragged her in his arms, slanted his lips over hers and kissed her so deeply that her heart completely melted.

THE VOICE INSIDE SLADE'S head whispered for him to stop the kiss, but he ignored it. Nina deserved one night of love, a night of pleasure to help her forget all the anguish she'd suffered. And he intended to give it to her.

Her lips tasted like warm sunshine, her purr of arousal as he teased her lips apart with his tongue sending fire straight to his sex. He wanted her more than he'd wanted a woman in a long time.

Maybe more than he ever had.

And not just because of her sexy body. Because he admired her, even liked her.

The emotions pummeling him made her kisses more special, more erotic.

Made him wonder if he'd be able to walk away when the case was over.

Of course, he would. He wasn't a settle-down kind of man. He was a loner. Had to pay for not saving his mother and sister. For not being a better man.

She made a low, throaty sound of need, and he deepened the kiss, threading his fingers into her hair and savoring the erotic scent of her skin as he dipped his head lower to taste her throat. He didn't deserve her or a family, not after his failures.

But he would take tonight for both of them.

He spread kisses around her face, down her

neck, dipping his head toward her cleavage, and cupping one breast in his palm.

A surge of excitement shot through him as her nipple stiffened beneath his touch.

That damn satin robe clung to her curves, leaving little to the imagination, but he still wanted more. He wanted it off, her bare skin against his, her body wrapped around his own.

A moment of sanity gripped him, and he realized they were standing in the hall in front of the stairs. He didn't want her on the cold floor—he wanted her in bed lying beneath him.

His heart racing, he swung her up into his arms and climbed the stairs. She clung to him, kissing him greedily, teasing his ear with her tongue then tracing a damp path down his neck where her fingers tugged at the buttons on his shirt.

Hungry for her, he lowered her on the bed, his breathing slashing the silence in the room. The rain had died, and a sliver of moonlight wove through the sheers, illuminating her like an angel lying on the sheets, an angel offering herself to him.

She licked her lips in a devilish grin, her fingers struggling with the buttons. He was tempted to rip the damn thing off, but forced himself to wait. To watch the stormy play of colors in her eyes as she smiled at him, to savor the feel of her fingertips grazing his chest as she slid open the folds of the shirt. Then her hands raked over him, greedily, and she reached for his zipper. His sex was straining to be free, but he caught her hand.

"Not yet. I want to see you first," he murmured. Heat seared his blood as he tugged the belt of her robe and opened the satin so he could feast on her naked breasts. They lay like golden globes waiting for him to hold, her nipples taut and rosy in the moonlight, and he lowered his head and traced his tongue over one gorgeous tip, then the other.

She moaned and thrust her hips upward, making his erection strain against his fly. Smiling, he sucked one taut bud into his mouth and suckled her, then rolled the other between his fingers, teasing and taunting her until she groaned his name.

"Please, Slade…" Her fingers fumbled with his belt, and he let her remove it this time, then he stepped back, slipped her robe the rest of the way off and allowed himself the sheer pleasure of looking at her naked and waiting for him on the bed.

A blush stained her cheeks, but she didn't cover herself, she simply let him look his fill.

"You're so damn beautiful," he whispered hoarsely.

"Take off your jeans," she ordered, one eyebrow lifting as she propped herself on her elbows. "I want to watch."

So sweet, vulnerable Nina could be demanding in bed. He shouldn't be surprised. She was a woman who went after what she wanted, and damned if he knew why, but she wanted him.

And he was determined to give her what she wanted. *Everything* she wanted.

At least for tonight.

So he slowly lowered his zipper, the rasp of it crackling in the tension-laden air, then grabbed a condom from his pocket before meeting her back on the bed. She reached for him and he fell into her arms, then kissed her again, deeper, more intimately, tasting the heady scent of her arousal as he dipped down to tease her breasts again, then lower over her belly and to the sweet, honeyed flesh between her thighs.

She was moist with desire, and he breathed in her essence then licked and teased her legs apart until his mouth closed over her sex, swollen with want and need.

A second later, she moaned his name and her body convulsed, the succulent taste of her release flooding his throat. Breathing like a wild man, he lifted his head and stared at her for a moment. Her cheeks were flushed with pleasure, her eyes glazed and hungry.

She wanted more and so did he.

He tore the condom wrapper open with his teeth, and she helped him sheathe himself, then he gripped her hips and teased her legs apart again with his sex. She closed her eyes and groaned, and he lowered his head and kissed her again, then thrust into her. She was small and tight, and he wondered momentarily if she'd been with another man since that creep William, then knew without asking that she hadn't.

The fact that she'd allowed him this guilty pleasure moved emotions deep inside him, emotions he didn't want to feel or face.

But he felt them anyway, just as he felt her delicious body hugging him inside her, felt her muscles clench and tighten around him. She clung to his arms as he thrust deeper inside her, then pulled out and thrust again and again until she rocked her hips upward, matching his rhythm, and they soared to the heavens together.

NINA SNUGGLED UP TO SLADE, her body humming with bliss. Slade wrapped his arms around her, and stroked her hair, his breathing heavy in the silence.

She pressed her face against his chest, savoring the euphoria rippling through her body. Emotions welled in her chest and throat and a tear spilled over.

Slade lifted her head back and searched her face. "What's wrong, Nina?"

"I think I'm falling in love with you," she whispered.

Slade tensed, and immediately withdrew from her.

"Slade?"

He sat up, swung his legs over to the side and leaned his head into his hands. She'd made a mistake in blurting out her feelings, but their lovemaking had touched her down to her soul.

She stroked his back, coaxing him to face her. "I'm sorry. I didn't mean that to pressure you."

He angled his head and stared at her, but he was shutting down in front of her eyes, and the hunger she'd seen earlier had vanished. "Nina, you don't love me. You're just grateful that I've been helping you—"

Anger knotted her stomach. "I didn't make love to you out of gratitude."

"You're coming off an adrenaline rush,"

he said matter-of-factly. "We both are. We almost died tonight." He gestured toward the rumpled sheets. "That's all this was."

Hurt stabbed Nina, but before she could reply, the doorbell rang.

Slade narrowed his eyes in question, and she clenched the sheets. "I wonder who that is this time of night."

"Maybe the sheriff." Slade stood, grabbed his jeans and shirt and hurriedly dressed. "I'll go find out."

Nina waited until he left the room, then grabbed a pair of shorts and a shirt and tugged them on, and ran a brush through her hair. She heard a woman's then a man's voice from downstairs, then Slade's and rushed down the steps.

She was shocked to see Gwen and Roan Waldorp in the doorway. Gwen's eyes were red-rimmed and swollen, and her husband looked angry.

"Nina, they said they have to talk to you," Slade said.

Dread mushroomed inside Nina. Something was wrong, and she had a sinking feeling it had to do with her daughter.

Chapter Seventeen

Slade must have sensed that she was falling apart, because he guided her to the living-room sofa, indicating for the couple to follow.

When they were all seated, Nina blinked, forcing herself to calm down and listen to what they had to say.

"Why did you come?" Slade asked bluntly.

Gwen glanced at her husband, and he cradled her hand in his. Gwen gripped it as if she needed a lifeline.

"I'm sorry," Gwen whispered. "We... I wanted to tell you that day you came to the house, but I...was afraid...and ashamed."

"Then we heard the news about Dr. Emery's arrest," Waldorp said. "And we knew we had to come forward."

"Because you were afraid of being arrested, too?" Slade asked coldly.

Gwen shook her head. "Because it was the right thing to do."

Nina inhaled a deep breath. "What are you talking about?"

Gwen glanced down at her lap where she was clenching her husband's hands. "We were supposed to adopt your baby."

Nina's heart raced. "What do you mean, you were *supposed* to?"

"After we lost our child, we paid Stanford Mansfield to find us another one," the husband said. "He said he'd let us know when a baby became available."

Slade sat down beside Nina and placed a comforting hand on her shoulder. "Then what?"

"He called a couple of weeks later, and said he'd found a little girl, that her mother abandoned her and she needed someone to adopt her."

"He told you I abandoned her?" Nina said, furious.

Gwen nodded then lifted her head and looked at Nina again. "We honestly didn't know she was your baby. We believed him."

"So he brought my little girl to you?" Nina asked.

"Yes," Roan said.

Gwen's lip trembled. "I'm so sorry, Nina. And so ashamed…"

Nina bit down on her lower lip. "Ashamed? Why?"

"Because we…saw her, and she was so frail and needed physical therapy…so we decided we couldn't keep her." Gwen swiped back a tear that trickled down her cheek. "We didn't know how to handle a handicapped child."

Slade squeezed Nina's shoulder. "What did you do then?"

"We explained our misgivings to Mansfield," Roan said, then gave Nina a pleading look. "You have to understand. We lost one child, and we wanted a perfect one…"

Nina nearly came off the chair. She wanted to scream at them to leave, to tell them they were cruel, but she'd forced herself to school her emotions for so long, that she managed to rein in her temper.

"So what happened to Nina's baby?" Slade asked.

"We have no idea," Waldorp said. "I assumed someone else adopted her, and a week later, Mansfield phoned that he had another child for us."

"We had no idea she was your baby back then," Gwen said shakily. "I was so traumatized from our own ordeal that it never occurred to us that Mr. Mansfield had lied about the mother."

"And when we came to see you the other day?" Slade asked.

Gwen and her husband exchanged a wary look. "We put it all together and we were afraid," Gwen said in a low voice.

"Afraid Nina would blame you?" Slade asked. "That you'd lose your daughter?"

Gwen and Roan nodded miserably. "And that you'd think we had something to do with the kidnapping," Roan said. "But we didn't."

Nina understood their fear, and had no idea if it was founded. All she could think about was that this couple had rejected her daughter.

How else had Peyton suffered? And where was she now?

In a home or somewhere lost, alone, feeling abandoned?

SLADE STRUGGLED TO control his rage as the couple left. They wanted a *perfect* child.

Peyton hadn't been perfect.

So if they had given birth to a handicapped child, what would they have done—given that baby away, too?

Nina obviously didn't feel that way.

Dammit. He wanted to put her child back in her arms so badly he could taste it.

"Nina?"

"I don't understand people like them," Nina said, her voice laced with sadness.

Just as he couldn't believe it when his own mother had dropped him off on the doorstep of the orphanage and never returned...

"Not everyone is as strong as you, Nina."

She gave a bitter laugh. "Me? You're forgetting that I'm the one who had the breakdown."

"Under the circumstances, having an emotional breakdown was understandable. You'd not only lost a child, but someone tormented you with that loss." He breathed out deeply to keep from touching her. "I'm going to make some phone calls."

She nodded, but she looked numb as she walked over, picked up the picture of her baby and stared at it. He imagined the train of her thoughts, and forced himself to block out his ping-ponging emotions.

He stepped into the kitchen and punched in the sheriff's number. "It's Slade Blackburn. The Waldorp couple just stopped by and admitted they were supposed to adopt Peyton Nash, that she was alive after that fire. But they declined to keep her because she was handicapped. They also confirmed that Stanford Mansfield handled the adoptions. Have you found him yet?"

"No, I checked his house and it looks like he left in a hurry. I have an APB out on him now."

"Let me know when you track him down. He might be able to lead us to Peyton."

He disconnected the call, then phoned Gage and asked him to have Ben Camp find out if Mansfield had a second house or vacation spot where he might be hiding out.

Then he spoke to Derrick McKinney and explained the latest revelations in the case.

When he ended the call, Slade pocketed his phone then went back to the living room.

Her gaze met his, tension thrumming between them. "I'm going to lie down."

He stared at her for a long moment, the memory of their lovemaking taunting him. He wanted to go back to bed with her.

But she had declared her love and he had thrown it in her face, so he knew he couldn't join her.

Still, he wouldn't give up.

He had to find Peyton for her. He couldn't fail her as he had his sister and mother.

Nina lay awake, restless and emotionally wrought. She found herself hating the Waldorp couple for giving her daughter back. If they'd kept her in Sanctuary, she might have recognized her, discovered where she was sooner.

All these years wasted.

Stop it, she reminded herself. *When you find her, you'll make up for lost time.* That is, *if* she found her. If she had been adopted, she might never be able to locate her. The people could have moved anywhere, even out of the country....

And if she hadn't? How had her little girl suffered?

Downstairs, she heard Slade moving around and prayed he'd come upstairs, crawl into bed and hold her.

But like so many other times, her prayers went unanswered.

Slade had slept with her because she was available and needy. God, he'd probably felt sorry for her.

Embarrassment flooded her and she vowed not to throw herself at him again.

She'd survived all these years alone. She would survive now.

She closed her eyes and focused, tried to hear her little girl singing to her. But the sound of a child's crying echoed in her head instead.

Peyton was lost and lonely and needed her mommy....

She climbed from bed and retrieved the tiny dress she'd bought years ago and inhaled the scent. Then she crawled back into bed, buried her head in the covers and sobbed her heart out.

Finally dawn streaked the sky, and she forced her achy body from bed and showered. Her face looked puffy, her eyes red-rimmed and swollen, and she made a futile attempt to cover the splotches with powder.

What difference did it make how she looked? Slade wasn't waiting downstairs to tell her he loved her.

She dressed in jeans, a cotton T-shirt and sandals and headed down the steps for coffee. Slade was sitting at the table with a cup already. His gaze met hers, deep and probing, and she wondered if he'd heard her crying.

But if he did, he didn't mention it. "I'm going to the jail to question Emery."

She poured herself a cup of coffee and sipped it. "I'll go with you."

For a moment, he looked as if he intended to tell her no, but she needed to see this through and would refuse to take no for an answer.

The storm clouds from the night before still lingered, painting the sky a dismal, dreary gray and adding a chill to the mountain air that sent a shiver through her as she stepped outside. Traffic was light, but a few shopkeepers were starting to open up, and the diner looked packed with the breakfast crowd.

Slade parked in front of the sheriff's office, and they headed inside silently. Her ankle still ached, but she managed to walk inside without reaching for Slade for help.

No more doing that. Keep it professional.

But as soon as they entered the front office, Nina knew something was wrong. The medical examiner was standing in the front talking to Sheriff Driscill in a hushed voice.

They glanced up, both looking haggard, and the sheriff shook his head as if in disgust.

"What's going on?" Slade asked.

Driscill blew out an exasperated breath. "Dr. Emery is dead."

"What?" Nina gasped.

The medical examiner ran a hand through his gray hair. "He committed suicide sometime in the night. Hanged himself with his own belt and tie."

SLADE GLANCED AT NINA'S pale face and cursed. The damn coward had known he'd rot in jail, and couldn't face it. But he'd taken his secrets with him to his grave.

No…maybe not.

"Sheriff, did you get a subpoena for his files? He may have kept a database of the adoptions he arranged."

"I've put in a request," Sheriff Driscill said.

Slade's phone buzzed, and he glanced at the number. GAI. Maybe they had a lead.

"I need to get this." Nina gave him an inquisitive look, and he stepped outside to answer the phone.

"Blackburn, this is Derrick. I just talked to Brianna, and you won't believe this. We may have a lead on Peyton."

"What?"

"The social worker Nina knows called and there's a little girl who was just turned back into the system. She's been in foster care for years, has vision problems, and her latest foster parents say they can't take care of her."

"When and where was she born?"

"Sanctuary Hospital, eight years ago."

Slade scribbled down the address and

disconnected the phone, then turned to Nina. He hoped to hell this little girl was her child, and that she wouldn't have to face another disappointment.

REBECCA HUGGED HER rag doll to her chest, rocking her back and forth, as she sat huddled on the cot in the orphanage. A big girl with a bulldog face stared at her as if she didn't want her around, and downstairs a little boy was crying.

The place smelled dusty and a spider had spun a web above her bed on the dirt-coated window.

"So those people didn't want you?" the girl said with a snarl.

Rebecca shook her head, but clutched the doll tighter.

"You'd better get used to this place," the girl said. "No one wants kids who ain't normal."

Tears pushed at the back of Rebecca's eyes. The girl was right. The old lady had said the same thing. She'd called her a freak, said she knew why no one had ever kept her.

Why no one ever would.

The bulldog-faced girl barreled from the room, leaving her alone, and Rebecca toyed with her doll's pigtails. The doll looked so sad that Rebecca swayed her side to side like a baby. She wanted to sing to her, but her throat wouldn't work, and she was afraid if she tried, she'd start crying.

Chapter Eighteen

Nina's pulse clamored as they drove to the orphanage in the mountains. Slade had phoned the social worker and asked for all of the records of the little girl to verify that she was Peyton.

So far, the paper trail indicated she was. But DNA would have to be checked to make certain.

The tension that had riddled the air between them ever since they'd made love intensified as they neared the concrete building and parked.

"Nina," Slade said in a thick voice, "if this—"

"Don't," she said, cutting him off. "I know this little girl may or may not be mine. And maybe I won't even know, won't recognize her, but I have to do this."

He stared at her for a heartbeat, then nodded and they climbed out and walked up to the door in silence. Slade knocked, and a plump middle-aged woman with curly hair opened the door.

"I'm Mildred, the house mother," the woman said with a friendly smile. "Brianna McKinney phoned and explained the circumstances and said that you were coming."

Nina cleared her throat, willing herself to be strong when her legs felt like rubber. "Where is the little girl?"

"Up in the dorm room," Mildred said. "Poor little thing has hardly said a word since she arrived. The man and woman who brought her here weren't very nice."

Anguish squeezed Nina's chest, robbing her of breath.

"Can we talk to her?" Slade said.

"Of course." Mildred placed a hand on Nina's arm. "But please… She's been shuffled around a lot. Be gentle with her. I'm not sure how much more the little thing can handle."

Tears threatened to choke Nina, and she couldn't speak. She simply nodded, and she and Slade walked into the office to the right, sat down on the couch and waited while the woman climbed the wooden steps to retrieve the little girl. Anger at the system filled Nina. Her daughter or not, no child should have to suffer and not feel loved or wanted.

Seconds later, the wooden steps creaked, and a tiny girl with sandy-blond pigtails appeared in the doorway, wearing a faded dress that looked two sizes too large for her slender frame. Freckles dotted her nose and she pushed her thick glasses up on her face. She looked timid and scared, and so damn small and unhappy that Nina's heart melted.

"Peyton?"

The child scrunched her nose. "My name is Rebecca."

"Her papers say Rebecca Davis," Mildred interjected.

Nina forced herself to breathe. "Hi, Rebecca." She glanced at Slade, then spoke in a low whisper. "Davis is William's middle name."

His look hardened. "Then William has more questions to answer."

Nina spotted the rag doll in Rebecca's arms, and smiled. "I like your doll. What's her name?"

Rebecca chewed her bottom lip for a moment, then lifted her chin bravely. God help her. Nina wanted to sweep her in her arms and hug her.

"Pippi."

Nina smiled. "After Pippi Longstocking?"

Rebecca slowly nodded. "You know Pippi?"

"She's my favorite." Nina rose, slowly walked over and stooped down to Rebecca's eye level. "I have all the Pippi Longstocking books. I collected them when I was your age, and I read them to my second-grade class every year."

Rebecca pushed her glasses up on her nose again. "Really?"

"Really," Nina said. "When I was little, I used to want to be just like Pippi."

Rebecca's head bobbed up and down. "Me, too."

Nina stroked the doll's pigtails. "I like Mary Poppins, too. I always sing along with the songs. Do you like to sing?"

That wary look crossed her face again. "Yes," she said in a tiny voice. "But the people I stayed with didn't like it."

Protective instincts surged through Nina. She was almost certain this little girl was her long-lost child. But even if she wasn't her blood relative, she would take her home and love her anyway. "Come and sit with me and let me tell you a story."

She reached out her hand and Rebecca slid her small hand inside hers. Trusting but wary.

Nina's chest threatened to explode as she led Rebecca to the sofa. They sat down, her hand still holding Rebecca's.

She felt an instant connection, felt the emptiness inside her bursting with love and happiness. But she didn't want to frighten Rebecca.

Keeping her voice to a soothing pitch, she began, "A long time ago, eight years to be exact, I had a baby girl. But that night there was a terrible fire at the hospital where she was born. I got lost from her, and I've been looking for her ever since."

"I losted my mommy, too." Rebecca sighed. "Did you ever find your little girl?"

"I think so," Nina said softly. "I used to hear her sing to me at night. Do you know what song she would sing?"

Hope lit up the little girl's big blue eyes. "Mary Poppins—"

"Just a spoonful of sugar," Nina said, her throat thickening.

Rebecca gasped. "You heard me?"

Nina nodded, and tears filled her eyes. "Oh, honey, yes, I heard you." She raked a strand of Rebecca's hair from her forehead. "And I want you to come home and live with me forever."

Rebecca's lower lip quivered. "But everybody says I'm too much trouble." Her sweet voice cracked. "I have to have special help in school…and I take medicine for seizures."

Nina wanted to scream and shout and cry against all the injustice her daughter had suffered. "You are the most beautiful little girl I've ever seen," Nina whispered. "And I want to be your mommy forever."

Then she did what she'd wanted to do for years. She pulled her daughter into her arms and hugged her.

EMOTIONS CHOKED SLADE every time he replayed the reunion between Nina and her daughter in his head. Finally Nina had her child, and they could make a family.

A family he would not be a part of.

He clenched his jaw, reminding himself that he didn't want to be part of it. That he liked being alone.

But at night in his big, empty house the past two days, he found himself imagining the pitter-patter of little feet racing across the floor in the morning. Imagined Rebecca running into the bedroom where he and Nina lay cuddling.

Imagined Nina pregnant, her belly swollen with his own child. A brother or sister for Rebecca.

Dammit, he missed Nina. He even missed the little girl and he barely knew her.

Shoving those foolish images out of his mind, he headed toward the sheriff's office.

He'd finally convinced Driscill to bring William Hood and his mother in for questioning on kidnapping charges. He'd also requested Nina's father be present.

Any one of them could have grabbed Rebecca that night—or collaborated together.

But he hadn't told Nina about the meeting. He wanted to spare her.

He entered the sheriff's office, prepared to pound the truth out of the Hoods or Nash, but Nina's father looked distraught already.

"You're telling me that Nina's child did survive the fire?" Nash asked.

Slade nodded. "DNA confirmed she's Nina's daughter."

"My God…" Nash collapsed into one of the wooden chairs. "Nina was right all along… and all this time I didn't believe her." His voice choked. "I thought she just couldn't handle the grief."

"Someone very cruel kidnapped the child, then taunted her by leaving gifts and children's things in her house to drive her over the edge," Slade said stonily.

Nash buried his face in his hands. "Oh, my

God, Nina tried to tell me… She must hate me…"

William's face paled. "Where has the child been all this time?"

Slade glared at him and his mother. "Don't pretend like you don't know. One or both of you arranged to have her kidnapped from the hospital. Either that or when the fire broke out, you saw the perfect opportunity."

William shot up. "Look, I admit that I didn't want the baby, but I didn't kidnap her. I honestly thought she died in that fire."

Mrs. Hood fumbled with her hands, and Slade angled himself to her. "But you did know, didn't you?"

"That girl and her illegitimate child were going to ruin our family!" she shrieked.

William suddenly turned on his mother with a shocked look. "Mother, what did you do?"

"I didn't do anything," Mrs. Hood cried. "Except to think of you."

"Mother," William spat out, "what happened?"

Mrs. Hood raked a strand of silver hair from her cheek, her diamonds glittering. "Nothing that was so horrible, so don't look at me like that. I simply paid Stanford Mansfield to arrange an adoption. The baby was supposed to go to a nice young couple who could raise her, one with two parents."

"The Waldorps," Slade filled in. "But when they realized the little girl was handicapped, they decided they didn't want her either."

Mr. Nash jerked his head up. "Then what happened to her?"

"They put her in foster care," Slade said, rage eating at him. "She's been shuffled from one place to another all these years, while you all ignored Nina and her."

Nash paced across the room, his expression miserable. Slade was glad to see that he did care about his daughter. Maybe they could reconcile.

But Mrs. Hood showed no regrets.

Slade turned on her. "Did you steal the baby or did you hire someone?"

The woman's hawklike eyes gleamed. "I refuse to say another word until I have an attorney."

NINA HUNG UP THE PHONE, her emotions on a roller coaster. Getting to know her daughter, shopping for furniture and bedding to decorate her room, laughing and watching movies and cuddling at night had been pure bliss. She couldn't wait until the four-poster white bed she'd ordered arrived and saw

Rebecca snuggled up, sleeping under the lacy canopy.

Although occasionally her anger and sadness over the years they'd lost surfaced, she refused to dwell on it. They'd finally found each other and she would never be separated from her daughter again.

She scraped her hand through her hair, staring at the phone in dismay. And now her father had called. He'd apologized for not believing her before, for letting her down, and wanted to make it up to her and her daughter. She'd declined his offer of money, but was overjoyed to know that he wanted to be a grandfather, that he would be a part of her family.

The only thing missing was Slade.

He thought she'd mistaken gratitude for love, but he was wrong. She loved him deeply.

Enough to let him go.

Not every man wanted a ready-made family, especially one with challenges to face.

Rebecca suddenly appeared at the bottom of the steps in her new pink pajamas. "Tuck me in, Mommy."

Nina smiled and took Rebecca's small hand in hers, and they walked to her bedroom. Rebecca climbed in bed and hugged her rag doll, and Nina crawled in bed beside her, then sang to her until Rebecca's eyelids drooped and she drifted asleep. Even then, she lay and watched her daughter for a while, soaking in the fact that she finally had her home.

Finally she fell into a deep sleep, content and dreaming of her first Christmas to come with her daughter home.

But sometime later, she woke to the acrid scent of smoke wafting toward her. A second later, the fire alarm downstairs blared.

Panic assaulted her, and she jumped up and ran to the steps. Dear heavens, the foyer was on fire.

The flames were spreading quickly, eating up the living room and front of the house, completely blocking her path to the door. Smoke clogged her lungs as she raced up the steps.

She had to get Rebecca out.

With one hand, she grabbed the phone and punched 9-1-1. With the other she gently shook her daughter. Smoke was rising and seeping into the hallway, wood crackling downstairs.

The 9-1-1 operator answered. "My house is on fire," Nina said, then recited her address and dropped the phone, pulling Rebecca into her arms. "Wake up, sweetie. We have to get out of here."

Rebecca stirred and rubbed her eyes. "Mommy?"

"Honey, there's a fire downstairs. We have to get out."

Her mind raced for an escape route. The only way out was downstairs, but they couldn't make it through the blaze. They'd have to climb through a window.

Rebecca coughed. "Mommy, I'm scared…"

"I know, sugar." Nina stroked her hair. "But I'll take care of you, I promise." She had to. She couldn't lose her little girl again.

She glanced out the window in her room, but there was nothing to hold on to outside the window, no ledge, no tree, nothing. Pulse pounding, she buried Rebecca's head against her chest to keep her from inhaling smoke and ran to the room she planned to paint for her daughter.

A huge oak tree stood beside the house, its branches massive, one limb touching the glass pane. She and Rebecca had talked about building a tree house in it.

"I'm going to sit you down, honey, and open the window," Nina said. "Then we're going to crawl into the tree. When the firemen arrive, they'll rescue us."

Rebecca's eyes widened. "I can't climb a tree, Mommy."

Nina hated the sound of her daughter's fear and uncertainty, but smoke was beginning to curl into the room, and glass downstairs shattered as the fire spread.

She stooped down and stroked her arms. "Rebecca, remember the story we read last night about the little engine that could?"

Rebecca's head bobbed up and down. "The little engine didn't think he could make it—"

"But he said, 'I think I can, I think I can,' and he did," Nina whispered. "That's what we have to do now."

"All right." Rebecca's chin lifted again, and Nina's heart swelled. Her child wasn't handicapped. She was the bravest, most special little girl in the world.

"Ready?" Nina asked.

Rebecca nodded, and Nina pushed open the window and lifted her in her arms. "Just grab that branch, sweetie, wrap your arms around it and hang on."

Rebecca tried, but her arms were too weak, and Nina gasped as she missed and nearly plunged downward.

Fear threatened to immobilize her, but she refused to give up. She hadn't searched all these years for her child only to lose her now.

She hugged Rebecca to her. "Listen, sweetie, I'm going to climb first, then pull you up."

Rebecca tugged at her arm. "No. Don't leave me, Mommy."

Tears filled Nina's eyes, and she cradled Rebecca's small face between her hands. "Sweetheart, I love you. I will never leave you, you understand?"

Rebecca's chin quivered, but she finally nodded.

Smoke was growing thicker, and the blaze had inched up the steps and was eating at the wooden doorway of the bedroom.

They had to hurry.

She kissed Rebecca's cheek, then released her and dragged a chair to the window. She climbed in the chair, then lifted Rebecca up beside her. Then she hoisted herself through the window. She was shaking all over, but gripped the limb with all her might, testing it to make sure it would hold them.

Satisfied it would, she reached for her daughter. "Come on, sweetie."

Rebecca stood on tiptoes in the chair and held up her arms. "I think I can, I think I can..."

Nina grabbed her and hauled her up beside her. It took every bit of concentration for her to steady them, but she wrapped Rebecca beneath her, and held on for dear life.

FEAR STABBED SLADE AS he raced up Nina's drive. He'd been at the sheriff's waiting on Mrs. Hood's lawyer when the 9-1-1 call had come in.

He'd run out and nearly had a heart attack as he'd driven to her house, afraid he would be too late.

Afraid he might lose her.

God, he loved her....

He couldn't let her go. And he sure as hell couldn't let her die....

Behind him, a siren wailed, but he beat the fire engine to the house, threw the vehicle into Park, jumped out and raced toward the house. The fire was blazing, the entire front burning wildly, smoke floating in a thick plume.

Where was Nina? Had she and Rebecca escaped?

Frantically he shouted her name over and over as he ran to the side of the house, searching the windows to see if she was trapped inside.

"Nina!" he shouted. "Nina, where are you?"

Wood crackled and popped, glass shattering as the porch collapsed and the fire spread upward. He coughed, the heat scalding him as he checked the back of the house. On fire, too.

Slade shouted Nina's name again, then Rebecca's. Frantically, he raced to the other side of the house and checked the guest bedroom window. It was ajar and flames shot through the opening.

Panic nearly made him collapse. There was no way they could survive....

Chapter Nineteen

"Slade!"

The fire engine wailed closer, but Slade was certain he'd heard Nina. Where the hell was she?

Suddenly a low, keening sound echoed from somewhere above. The tree branch shook. Leaves rained down.

"Nina?"

"Slade! We're up here! Hurry!"

Slade frowned and peered through the fog of smoke, then spotted Nina cradling her daughter huddled on a tree branch.

Thank God they were alive.

"Hang on, I'll be right there." He studied the tree, gauging his path, then grabbed the lowest branch and hurled himself upward. He climbed as quickly as possible, testing each branch as he climbed to make sure it would hold him.

Rebecca looked pale in the light of the

blaze, and both she and Nina were sweating from the heat. One branch, two, another… He climbed until he made it to the branch below them.

"Take Rebecca down first," Nina cried.

Slade's gaze met hers, and he knew that she was afraid the branch was going to catch on fire. The flames were inching out the window toward her.

"I'm going to get you both down," he said through gritted teeth.

"Please, Slade, take her," Nina whispered.

"Mommy, I don't want to leave you," Rebecca sobbed.

"I'll be right behind you," Nina said softly. "I promise."

Rebecca's fingers tightened around her for a second, then Slade stroked her hair.

"Rebecca, honey, listen to me. I'm going to save you and your mommy, but you have to trust me."

Terror darkened her eyes as she clung to Nina. "Mommy…"

Nina lifted her daughter's chin and forced her to look at her. "You can trust Slade, honey. I'll be right behind you, I promise. But we have to hurry."

Rebecca bit down on her lip. "'Kay."

Slade smiled at her. "That's good, honey.

Now I want you to climb on my back, and wrap your arms around my neck like a monkey. Then put your legs around me, too, and hold on as tight as you can."

"Remember the little engine," Nina said softly.

Nina helped her daughter wind her arms around his neck, then Rebecca squeezed her little legs to his waist, and he began climbing down.

The fire engine finally arrived and careened to a stop, and he shouted for them to help him. The men jumped into motion. Two men dragged a hose to douse the flames while another spotted him as he dropped to the ground with Rebecca and raced over with a ladder.

"I'll get Nina, you try to save the house," Slade shouted. He didn't wait on a response, but gripped the ladder and began climbing. Nina was trying to make her way down, but slipped and dangled from a branch above him. Rebecca screamed, and Nina looked down, hanging on to the branch with one hand and clawing to reach it with the other.

"Hurry, I'm slipping," Nina cried.

"Hang on, honey." Slade grabbed her just before she plunged to the ground.

Fear shot through him as he pulled her to him, and he silently vowed never to leave her again. Then together they climbed down the ladder.

The firefighter helped her off the ladder first, then Slade jumped to the ground.

Nina pulled Rebecca into her arms, and the little girl clung to her, both of them trembling. He ushered them away from the heat of the burning house.

Another siren screeched, and suddenly the sheriff's car roared to a stop. Sheriff Driscill climbed out and strode toward them. Slade saw someone in the back of the squad car and frowned.

"You all okay?" Sheriff Driscill asked.

Slade nodded. "It was close, but yeah."

"I know who started the fire." Driscill jerked his thumb toward the car. "The same person who kidnapped the baby."

Nina pressed her daughter tighter into her embrace, and glanced at the police car. Slade saw the woman beating at the glass, screaming and crying.

"Mitzi…" Nina said in a stunned voice.

"I caught her racing away around the corner. She was hysterical, screaming that she had to do it. That she was afraid William would want you back now you found the child."

"William gave up his rights a long time ago," Nina said stiffly.

The sheriff nodded. "She also admitted that Hood's mother was in cahoots with her. Mitzi actually kidnapped the baby from the hospital, but Hood's mother paid for the adoption. They'll both serve time for this." He paused. "And one of my deputies found Mansfield. He's bringing him in, as well. He'll be charged with conspiracy."

Nina glanced at her house, the flames bursting higher.

"I'm sorry you lost the house," Slade said.

"It doesn't matter." Nina scooped Rebecca into her arms and hugged her. "I have all that's important right here."

Slade's resistance completely shattered. How could he not love a woman like her? She knew her priorities and fought for them.

"Thank you for saving us, Slade," she whispered.

He hesitated, remembered that he'd accused her of gratitude instead of love before, and shame filled him. He'd been a coward, had thought by punishing himself by being alone and denying himself happiness that he could atone for his guilt.

But Nina had taught him about courage. About really loving… "I don't want your gratitude, Nina."

Fire crackled and popped, illuminating her

beautiful face. But a puzzled look darkened her eyes. "Then what do you want, Slade?"

His throat thickened, and he knew he was taking a chance. Knew that he still might fail sometimes or lose them one day.

But he didn't want to lose them now.

"I want your love," he said in a husky voice.

A slow smile softened her mouth, and she placed a hand against his chest. "You have that already."

"And you have mine," Slade said gruffly.

Nina smiled, a radiant look that he knew would be imprinted in his mind forever. A look filled with love and hope and promises of a happily-ever-after.

Then she glanced down at her daughter, who was watching them with big eyes.

Slade gently stroked Rebecca's hair. "You have a mommy now, Rebecca. How would you feel about having a daddy, too?"

Her eyes lit up and she nodded wildly. Moved beyond speech, he wrapped his arms around both of them.

"I love you, Nina," he said against her hair. "And I will love you and your daughter forever, I promise."

"I love you, too," Nina whispered.

Then she closed her mouth over his and kissed him.

* * * * *

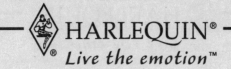
HARLEQUIN®
Live the emotion™

American ★ Romance®
Love, Home & Happiness

HARLEQUIN® *Blaze*
Red-hot reads.

Harlequin® Historical
Historical Romantic Adventure!

HARLEQUIN® *Romance®*
From the Heart, For the Heart

HARLEQUIN®
INTRIGUE
Breathtaking Romantic Suspense

Medical Romance™...
love is just a heartbeat away

HARLEQUIN®
Presents
Seduction and Passion Guaranteed!

HARLEQUIN® *Super Romance®*
Exciting, Emotional, Unexpected

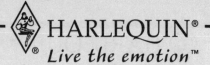

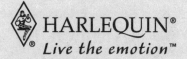

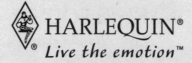

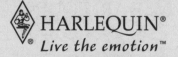

HARLEQUIN®
Presents

**The world's bestselling romance series...
The series that brings you your favorite authors,
month after month:**

Helen Bianchin...Emma Darcy
Lynne Graham...Penny Jordan
Miranda Lee...Sandra Marton
Anne Mather...Carole Mortimer
Melanie Milburne...Michelle Reid

and many more talented authors!

Wealthy, powerful, gorgeous men...
Women who have feelings just like your own...
The stories you love, set in exotic, glamorous locations...

Seduction and Passion Guaranteed!

HPDIR08

www.eHarlequin.com